Behind the Gate

RENEE ADAMS

Copyright

All rights reserved as permitted under the U.S. Copyright Act of 1976. No part of this publication may be reproduced, distributed, transmitted in any form or by any means, or stored in a database or retrieval system, without the prior permission of the Author. For information regarding subsidiary rights, please contact the publisher. This book is a work of fiction. Names, characters, places, and incidents are the product of the author's imagination or are used fictitiously. Any resemblance to actual events, locales, or persons, living or dead, is coincidental.

Cover Design by Silla Webb

Interior Design by Silla Webb

Editing by Silla Webb

http://www.alphaqueensbookobsession.blogspot.com/

Dedication

To my mom, Rhonda, who is the strongest cheerleader I know. You are the definition of the warden, but look at what has come from your warden like ways, I have a book now!

I hear him snicker as he takes his cereal bowl and sits it next to the empty sink then walks away to get dressed for the day. With a sigh, I put his bowl in the sink and make a mental note to talk to him about it tonight, for the sake of myself and his future wife.

He's a good kid who has had it rough after his dad walked out on us about two years ago. Not that his dad leaving was a huge upset to me, but to Jack it was because I guess he felt like he did something wrong. Of course he didn't, his dad just couldn't handle being a dad, and chased the little 18-year-old down the street a few states away. Jack spent a lot of time with my mom when I was going through nursing school, but I had to do it to better our lives. I knew he was scared because whenever I would pick him up from her house he had this look of relief like he didn't think I would come back. Of course I would, he is my rock star and my life, but I could still see the trepidation in his eyes when I would leave. My mom though is a saint for putting up with our crap for the last few years. Nursing school was hard, but it was worth it to provide a better life for us. Now, I work full time at the prison and things couldn't get better for me and my little man.

The prison, March Correctional Institute, although a very dangerous place to work at, has been good to us. My co-workers understand that I am a single mom and that Jack's dad is nowhere to be found. Some of them have even become like family to us. The prison itself is one of the worst in our state. We are a level three maximum security prison with a special death row unit. Our prison houses the worst of the worst, and it is my daily job to have in your face interaction with them. Of course, we have some weapons that we carry, and we are always wearing some kind of bulletproof vest and shield on our faces. Most of them treat us with respect, but that does not make them any less dangerous. I know that, but, I still go out of my way to make sure they are given a little bit of dignity.

After everything is ready and Jack has gotten his school stuff together, we make our way out the door. Jack goes to school right down the street so I get those mere few minutes alone with him before we head off to start our day. We sing along to some cheesy song that if the windows weren't rolled up Jack wouldn't sing along to.

"Have a good day, baby boy, learn something!" I yell as he is rushing to get out the car and away from his embarrassing mother. I like to embarrass him whenever I can. Even though he seems to hate it, I always wonder if that is real.

He runs down the car line, and I see him meet up with some friends and one very cute girl. He looks over at me and sees that I am still watching him, and he hangs his head in embarrassment. He knows he will get a "mom talk" tonight at bedtime. He's growing up so fast, and sometimes I wonder to myself whether he needs a man in his life to show him the man ropes. Sadly all he has is me and mom. We try our hardest, but sometimes we can't do it all in that department.

After stopping off for my morning soda, I head on to work. Every time I get close enough to see the barbed wire fence, I can't help but think back to my first interview there. Shaking in my shoes is an understatement, I thought for sure the warden, Rhonda, would hear my knees knock together. Once that gate closed behind me. I was petrified. I sat on a bench in the lobby and just kept looking at two things. The barbed wire and the metal detector. I was fresh out of nursing school and definitely green in my way of thinking. I always knew that I wanted to work in a prison because I am definitely far from the girly-girl type. But, being behind the fence walls made it all too real that this was a place that people have done bad things and were paying their price. I never forget that, every day that I work.

Walking up to the first gate and waiting for the front guard to buzz me in, it shakes me from my thoughts and takes that nervousness away. Already having worked here for a year, I get the nerves still but not nearly as bad as the first day. I give the guard, Teddy, my badge and he swipes it and tells me that there seems to be electricity in the air. I can feel it too after he says it and can't help but get a shiver down my spine. The last time I got that feeling, we had an inmate shank another and then try to attack the guards who were trying to get them under control. That incident cost me a pair of scrubs because they were covered in pepper spray from where the guards sprayed him. Let's just hope that today is not that kind of day. We do alright for ourselves, but we don't have money to just throw out whenever we want.

Saying my goodbyes to Teddy and going through the first gate, I head on to the metal detectors. I see a new guard whom I have never seen before manning the detectors, and I give a smile because he looks extremely nervous. Memories come back of my first day when I screwed up and didn't know all the rules yet. I tried to get my soda through with the label still on it. Luckily the guards were great and helped me along when it felt like my stomach was going to fall out of my butt!

We have a strict policy at the prison. Upon entry, we have to remove our shoes, of course, anything metal, and all outside food must be inspected. Once the pat down is done and I have my shoes on and things collected, I stand in front of the door and wait for the guy in the control room to open it for me. I can't see who is in there yet since I have to get through the door first, but as soon as the heavy door opens I see that it's Josh manning the controls today. He sits in his central location in front of a huge panel and monitors, watching everyone go about their day. His domain is the brains of the prison. He can see all cell blocks, the yard, and any other room that prisoners have access to. Making my way to be buzzed in the multiple doors, I think maybe it's time I take him up on his offer of a coffee date. He's been after me for months now, but he has a lot of hoops to jump through before I'll bring him around Jack. Stepping into the corridor between two doors, I am waiting for Josh to buzz me in when the loud speaker buzzes.

"Good morning, Olivia." Of course, it's Josh.

"Morning Josh, how's it going today?"

"Be even better if you let me take you on a date." I just laugh to myself, he is so shameless! See, there are those dimples that I like so much, come on just one date?"

"I'll think about it, now get back to work and buzz me through the door before you make me late!"

Making my way through the door and out into the walkway, I see the transport van going through the gate and know that today we are getting some new inmates. Medical has to check out every inmate that walks in, they are subject to blood draws for diseases, cavity searches for weapons and general health questions. It's long and tedious, but it helps us cut down on diseases through the inmate population. A lot of these guys are lifers so they depend on us to keep diseases out. Doesn't always work, but we try our hardest. Transport days always go one of two ways, good or bad, never the in between. The good inmates just let us get our job done without giving us problems, the bad are the ones who either don't give a shit or have something to prove like you always see in movies.

With a sigh, I reach the next door that I don't have to be buzzed in for and walk inside the medical ward, I immediately put on my face. Some call it the resting bitch face, I call it the "I don't take shit from anybody" face. It works for me, and most inmates will greet me with a "hi Olivia" and let me get on my way. Even though they have done some truly heinous things, it doesn't mean I have to be a bitch to them. I would like to think that me treating them as human beings and not garbage has saved my ass a time or two. Last year, we had a nurse get hit with a sock that had pieces of concrete that an inmate had been chunking off from the wall. Broke her nose and the lacrimal bone around her eye. That situation was my lesson learned. After that, I put on my resting bitch face or rbf for short, and it stays in place whenever I have any inmate interaction.

"Olivia, can you come here for a moment and help me?" A voice echoes through the room. Great. It's my boss, Mary. She's nice enough, although she doesn't take shit from anyone, inmate or employee. She has worked here for quite a while, and last month she was presented with a celebration of being the longest employee at the prison. Some 30 years or so, and she has no hard time bringing up the fact that she has been here since as some of us were in diapers. I wasn't born yet, but she doesn't seem to remember that.

"Let me put my stuff down first, then I'll be right in," I yell back. Mary is a nice lady when she wants to be and she perfected her rbf a long time ago.

"Of course, I'm in the med room, so come find me."

I put my stuff away in my designated cubby in the break room that only medical staff has key access to, then make my way to the med room. It's got one of those old-timey keys you see on movies, the big ones on the guards giant hoop keyring. There is only one key to this room, so we have to be extra careful with it. When the room is vacant we have to hold it on our body, but if the room is occupied we pass it through the slot underneath the bulletproof and shatterproof glass window. This where we keep all inmate medications, needles, scalpels, plus our gear. Our gear consists of a bulletproof/stab-proof vest, and a riot gear helmet with a spit shield. All of it combined weighs 13 pounds, so it's no wonder that I have lost 20 since working here.

Mary is crouched down on the floor filing the new meds into the inmate storage bins that. I can hear a few 'fuck this shit' come from her and chuckle because you know if you hear Mary cuss then something is really wrong.

"What's going on?" I ask her when I reach the window and wait for her to pass me the keys. On a start she nearly jumps out of her skin because she didn't hear me approach.

"Bitch, you almost gave me a heart attack!" she shouts as she passes me the keys.

Opening the door, I see all the meds scattered everywhere and immediately regret telling her I would be there to help. She's a nice lady but has a little problem with organization. It's going to take me hours to get all these meds organized. Luckily, I'll have some help once my other co-worker and seriously awesome friend Cori gets here. She is the light of my work day sometimes, and we can always make each other laugh. She is the only person who I see outside of work on a regular basis, she even helps me with Jack sometimes or comes over to share a bottle of booze with me. I guess she has kind of moved on to best friend territory.

"Today we have a big transport coming in, including a state to state transfer, so you will be busy today. I leave early so we called in Ryan to help you and Cori get through them all. A few violent ones, so be careful," Mary says and I groan because I would seriously think this is Monday instead of Friday with us having a big transport. Normally Mondays are our days to get new inmates.

I just shake my head at her because what the hell else am I gonna do? I've only worked with Ryan a handful of times, and even though he works somewhat hard, he still is smarmy as hell. He's somewhat handsy, but one day some girl is gonna get fed up with the creeper and kick him in the balls. Hell, it might just be me, and *that* will be a good day! He is one of those people who has to touch everyone he comes in contact with, like a subtle graze of the elbow or soft stroke of the hair. I can't stand people like that, and since I am short, he always ruffles the top of my head. Like I said, creeper and needs a kick in the balls. *One day.*

I hear a loud bang and have just enough time to look up to see a couple of unfamiliar guards bring in a line of inmates. The inmates are all cuffed at the wrist with a circle of thick chain wrapped at the waist that shackle their feet together. Linked at the center of the chain is a handle for the guards' convenience. At any point that an inmate is being treated, whether in medical or out in the yard, a guard will be holding that chain. It gives the inmate a little moving room but allows the guard to remain in control at all times in case the inmate becomes unruly. One yank and the inmate will be planted on his ass.

Seeing the inmates hobbling through the corridor in unison with guards at their side, I know the transport van is here and med organizing will have to wait. Mary instructs the guards where to place each inmate as we make our way out of the room and into the waiting room. The unnerving sense that I am being watched comes over me and it's enough to make the little hairs on the back of my neck stand up. I turn around and look down the line. I don't see anything out of the ordinary, even though dealing with inmates is way out of the ordinary for most regular people. I see the normal badass persona on each one of their faces, except one. I see the top of someone's head. Hmmm, maybe too many nights of watching crime shows on TV with Cori after Jack goes to bed has gotten to me.

I continue setting up for the inmate checks, and I run into a huge problem, well problem for me anyways. Being only 5'3 has its disadvantages, like now, when I have to reach for some paperwork.

"Need some help small stuff?' I hear behind me. I hate being called small stuff, short stack, little girl, you name it and I have probably been called that. When I was in school, I used to take karate on a weekly basis because my parents were scared I would get bullied for my short stature. I never did, I had a good personality that took me far. Cheerleading, dance, and all the typical stuff helped with popularity. Until I met Jack's dad that is and got pregnant my senior year of high school. Then I became the pregnant girl, and everyone seemed to forget who I was over night.

Gritting my teeth, I face the name caller and say, "Nope, all good," because I realize it's a guard I have only seen a few times. His name starts with a B, I think. Nice looking guy with a nice smile, even if he is a little older. Shit, I need to get laid. It has been since way before Jack's dad left that I last got some! Here I am thinking about hopping on a man I have never met before when my body instantly goes on alert because the feeling of being watched comes over me again.

I look around at the inmates and instead of seeing the top of someone's head this time I see a pair of bright blue eyes looking at me with contempt. Eyes that look like the water you see on commercials for faraway places I will never travel. Just a crystal clear blue staring back at me, his eyes full of a deep hatred. I dunno why, and honestly I don't care. But this man, he is the definition of sex, strong jaw, short black hair and those eyes. Aquamarine eyes would be the best way to describe them. The kind that can see your secrets and act as a human lie detector. My insides instantly start to heat up and boil to a mush, even though he is looking at me with absolute disgust. He is still the most breathtaking man I have ever seen. That whole 'I need to get laid' thought is dancing in my mind right now as my lady parts are screaming at me to jump on it. What a long flipping day this will be with Mr. Dark and Broody over there glaring at me. I redirect my attention to the task at hand silently hoping that Cori gets here soon. She can deal with Mr. Hateful eyes over here because I feel like if he keeps staring at me, I might catch fire from his hatred

"Did you hear what I said lady?" the guard asks.

"Yeah, and I said I didn't need your help, but thanks."

"No, about the transferred inmates," annoyance drips off of his words.

I must have dazed off in my cock-fueled day dreams and missed whatever this guy had to say. "I'm sorry, I missed it."

He looks even more annoyed but keeps giving a side-eye to Mr. Blue Eyes and Dangerous, because after looking over at him the guard seems to change his tone. It's then that I know that this Friday will be different from all the Fridays in the past.

The guard repeats about the transfers, something about one of them being extremely dangerous and we should make sure that we use extreme caution with him. I tune him out after that because blue eyes is looking my way with a knowing smirk as if he knew we were talking about him. The heated blaze of blood rushes to my cheeks making me blush. I feel like a heat lamp is shining down on me and turning me into a sweaty mess.

Around that time I hear Cori come in, grumbling about Starbucks ruining her order. She looks up when she realizes that all the guards' eyes are on her and instantly puts her face on and gets to work. I look back at the guards, they all look like they are drooling. Cori is beautiful and she knows it, but she's not a bitch about it.

I get supplies ready to get the inmates checked one by one, then I call out the first name: Xavier Richards. Scanning over the paperwork briefly, I see that he is in for aggravated assault with a deadly weapon, serving 27 months. He is a stocky man with tattoos running up and down his arms. Sigh, tattoos, love them and even have a few of my own, but I have to now catalog all of his tattoos for any discernable codes. Yes, that's right, codes. Some gang bangers will put codes onto their bodies before committing a crime that they are sent to do so they can funnel in codes for the higher ups in their gang that are serving time. Plus, this way, they know which unit to send him to because if he has gang-related tattoos then he cannot be put with other gangs.

The guard has a hold of his chain by the back and starts walking him over to where I am standing. I still feel like I am being watched, but work has to continue. I trust my co-workers to have my back, plus I have my "dick hit" tool in my pocket. It's the only weapon I am allowed to carry while inside the prison walls. It's plastic and looks like a dick head at the end, it's really just a throat punch, but Cori and I joke that it's the only dick I hold in my hands.

Xavier walks towards me and I automatically have a sense of unease that I can't explain. He seems nice enough, rough around the edges sure, but nice enough. I tell him and his guard to follow me, and we walk down the hall to the first exam room and shut the door.

"Y'all already got my shit so I dunno why I gotta come in here," he says.

"I gotta look at and write up about your tattoos, take some blood, and do a general exam."

"Y'alls dime, but shit, every time I come in here I gotta do this shit?"

"Stop breaking the law, asshole," the guard mumbles under his breath. I fake a cough to hide my laugh because the last thing any of us wants to do is get on an inmate's bad side.

Xavier glares at him. I try to diffuse the situation by getting back to work and start cataloging his extensive tattoo collection. Then I take some blood and get ready to finish up his exam when there is a loud bang on the other side of the door and people yelling. Sounds like a wrestling match out there, but it's not infrequent to hear a guard fighting with an inmate. But this time, something feels different, like the air in the room becomes static electricity. I hear a deep voice yelling and it seems to be getting closer to the room we're in. The guard looks slightly taken aback by the outburst going on outside our doors.

"Don't you need to go out there?" Xavier asks cooly, he seems smarmy like a snake.

The guard who I think is named Burton or Benton or something says, "Not unless they come fighting in here, then hell to the…" his words are cut off when the door burst open and guards and one inmate come tumbling through. Wouldn't you know it, it's blue eyes and he looks like he's ready for a fight. I shriek and grab my good ole dick hit and move to a corner. Xavier tries following but blue eyes lunges at him. In the melee I can hear blue eyes screaming something about, "he's taking too long," and, "he's gonna hurt her," but I have no idea who the 'her' is in his rant. With all of the crashing and thrashing that he is doing, I'm surprised Xavier isn't sitting in the corner with me.

There are now 5 guards, blue eyes and Xavier between me and the door. In reality, between me and Jack. Because I will fight tooth and nail to make it home to my baby boy.

Xavier creeps closer to me in my corner, a slight smile on his face like he just learned a secret. You would think a man in his position would be pissing his pants right now, but nope, he comes toward me and reaches out to me. Nobody tries to grab me! Before I realize it, Xavier is on the floor clutching his upper thigh. All that runs through my head is, "Ha the dick hit didn't hit the dick, but it still hurts. I'm a boss bitch now!" Before I can throw my fists in the air and do a little Rocky dance the crowd goes silent. Blue eyes isn't fighting anymore, just staring down at Xavier and shaking his head. The guards are working on getting blue eyes out the door when I realize that he burst through the door with his feet still in chains and his hands cuffed, albeit in front of him, but still cuffed.

Impressive? Yes.

Scary? Hell yes!

The guards haul him out of there and back into line to get checked out. We can't take him to his cell because of disease restrictions, so he has to wait his turn.

I glance over at the ground and Burton or Benton or whatever the guard's name is trying to help Xavier up. With him lying there writhing around I see that he is trying to say something. "You will pay for this bitch," and "I got your ass," are some of the things I can make out. Totally not scared of my job, but the way he is saying it and the look in his eyes has me pausing before I tell the guard to un-cuff him so that I can do his exam. I am a little leery about having him with no cuffs on, but I have a job to do. Benton/Burton hauls Xavier to his feet and proceeds to un-cuff and unshackle him.

"I'll keep the chain that wraps around his stomach and feeds to my handle." At that moment I could kiss whatever his name is.

Everything else is pretty unremarkable except the giant bruise I see on his thigh from my hit. I can't help but give a tight smile when I see it, I don't want Xavier to be set off by my happiness that I protected myself. Once done and dressed in his prison issue scrubs, the guard escorts him to his cell and the relief in me is immediate. I release the breath I didn't realize I was holding in. Most inmates don't scare me, but sometimes you get that one that gives you the creeps from the start. Xavier is one of them.

After finishing up with 3 other inmates in what feels like record time, I see that there is one left. Blue eyes himself. He looks a little worse for wear but still good enough to eat. He's tall, like I have to look up to him. Not hard when I am only 5'3, but this guy is very tall. He looks hard in all the right places with forearms that look like I could hang off of. I am a sucker for a nice, toned forearm. This guy just oozes sex even when he got into a fight earlier. I bet when he is not in prison women throw themselves at him. He is the type of guy that you want to climb like a tree and sit in his lap and let him use his God given talent to make a girl cream herself. Shit! I gotta tame the flames that are my vagina.

Once I call his name, Damian Shaw, I realize how much he looks like a Damian. The devil with blue eyes himself. He gets up and saunters towards me, even in shackles the man fucking saunters! My vagina is instantly on fire, and I have to send a "down girl" to her and send his image to my mental spank bank for later.

Escorting Damian and the 2 guards that are with him into the exam room, I feel his eyes on me. But instead of it putting me on alert for danger, this feels like a caress. Like soft hands are roaming down my back, or maybe it feels like little licks from a tongue, warm and soft. I am trying to get these thoughts out of my head when I look at him as he takes a seat and I realize that he doesn't have a guard chain. The one that feeds to a handle for the guard to hold. This worries me because I did just watch the guy go psycho a few hours ago. Even though he has 2 guards with him because of his earlier outburst, I still don't like that he doesn't have a chain.

"Why doesn't he have a guard chain?" questioning one of the guards whom I feel like I have seen before but don't quite remember.

"Does it fucking matter? Just do your job."

"Ha, someone had some rotten asshole at breakfast," I mutter under my breath. I look up to ask my first question and see Damian is staring straight at me with a perplexed expression. Like he is trying to understand me and keeps coming up short. At first I think he didn't hear me, but then he smirks and it is like looking at the Devil himself. An angel of sin, one that makes you want to do bad things, but love every minute of it.

"Damian, do you have any tattoos?"

"Enough."

"I need to see them please."

He just grunts at me like some caveman and stands. I instantly go on high alert and reach into my pocket for the dick hit. Just feeling the plastic and sliding my fingers into it and making my fist has me feeling better.

"Relax lady, I just need to get my shirt off."

I sort of feel embarrassed then think, 'eff that, he's psycho enough to kill me' and it's then I realize that I hadn't looked at his conviction. I always look at an inmate's crime, force of habit and morbid curiosity, but for some reason I didn't. I try not to read too much into it.

The guards un-cuff the Devil, I mean Damian, and he removes his shirt. I almost sigh when I catch sight of his washboard abs and the V. Lord help me the man has a V and a happy trail! I don't understand it because I have seen some seriously jacked dudes come through this clinic, but nothing has been more attractive than this man! My mouth goes dry like my body needs it for other places. Sitting down, I start the task of looking over his body, like it is a chore. He has a half sleeve on one arm, full of vibrant colors, and upon closer examination I realize that it is comic book characters. The whole sleeve is intricately designed, and probably took a lot of needle time. He has a few other tattoos, one that spans shoulder to shoulder. In script it says, "I am not afraid, I was born to do this," and I think about how the irony is strong in this one. Obviously not afraid to have landed him in this place. Another one on his side, this one says, "I desire the things which will destroy me in the end," and I almost chuckle out loud because my mind is running wild with the fact that he is now in prison and all of his worded tattoos are basically warnings saying 'don't worry I know it's gonna destroy me.' He has no gang affiliation tats on him unless he is in Wonder Woman's crew and there is a comic book gang going around.

"Is that all of them?"

"Yep,"

Well, ok king of the one word. Every time I go to write on his paperwork I can feel his eyes boring into me. Like he is assessing me as much as I am him. I go about collecting my blood draw supplies and apply the tourniquet to his arm, then I bite the finger of my glove off so I can feel for a vein. I am instantly greeted with a growl as I start running my finger over his bulging veins. Quick and easy, good stick, got the flash and I'm done, over in 5 minutes. Now comes the hard part. Gotta get him to strip down to his underwear so I can check him out, I mean exam him in a strictly medical way.

"Need you to strip to your underwear so we can finish up and you'll be on your way." I glance at the clock and realize that my shift is almost over. Really, 10 hours of inmate transfers? Sheesh no wonder I am feeling tired, it has been non-stop today! Luckily, I'm off this weekend and maybe Jack will let me sleep in. Fat chance of that, the kid has an internal alarm clock of six thirty.

Damian hasn't stripped yet, and I realize he is staring at me.

"Is there something wrong?"

"No."

"Well, then you need to get undressed."

He starts to take off the prison issue tennis shoes, then pants. If a thigh could be sexy, then this man has some sexy thighs. Big, but not tree trunk big. Just enough to complete the package that is Damian. As I continue my assessment of his perfect form, I notice the 2 back dimples that lead down to the most perfect ass. This is the kind of ass that would make any girl go bat shit crazy over. You want to just squeeze it and maybe bite a cheek or two. When he turns around, I see a semi hard erection in his boxer briefs. *Well then, Mr. Blue Eyes, nice to see that this is not a one way attraction.* I may or may not have dragged out looking at his body for my assessment.

I cannot believe I am standing here with my dick half hard in front of this woman! I mean what the hell is wrong with me? I'm in prison, but not by my own doing, and here I am lusting after this little pixie of a woman. Seriously, she comes up to right under my nipple. I don't need any kind of distraction while I am here, and this is all she will be.

She puts her warm hands on me, and I can't help but notice they are shaking a little. Is she scared of me? Other than earlier I have given her no reason to be scared of me. She has to know I was trying to protect her, and it had nothing to do with her really. That Xavier fucker is dangerous, plus you never know what guards he has in his back pocket. Prison workers, for the most part, aren't always what they seem to be. It's easy to buy things in here for the right price, or should I say the right payment. I should know, I have been to quite a few prisons. Half the fights and deaths in these kind of places aren't random or gang against gang like most think. Some of these are prison employee ordered hits.

As she continues on with her hands all over me, checking me over for other marks and identifiers, I have a minute to study her. She's short, like crazy short. I know I'm tall, I'm 6'6, but she has to be barely 5'4. Straight brown hair and huge brown eyes with a nice little petite nose and dimple when she smiles. I saw her smile when her friend walked in. Her teeth are straight, almost as if she has had braces, but I notice her teeth are a little crooked on the bottom. Enough to make it cute and adorable, not that she chewed rocks as a kid. I glance down at her hands and notice no wedding ring and no tan line where one might be. Interesting. When I get to her scrubs, which are plain, I notice her tits are more than a handful and I get excited even more. I say a silent prayer that I don't go full on hard in front of her, never mind the 2 guards, I couldn't give a shit about them. Don't need to scare the girl away. Sure, I'm cocky, but years of banging nameless women have made me that way. I know what I have between my legs, and I know how to use it to my advantage. You were going to leave satisfied after a few hours with me. That's for damn sure! If her scrub top is any indicator, she has a flat tummy and nice wide hips. The type of hips that you can hold onto when you are fucking her from behind. That ass of hers is damn near perfect. I would break this girl in half, even after I saw her defend herself against that scumbag Xavier. I still don't know how she got him down like that, and something tells me I don't want to either. But I don't think she realizes how crazy he is and that she may have put a target on her back.

"You're all done, you can get dressed and the guards will take you to your cell," her voice is a little breathy, like she had run a mile.

"Thanks."

So what? I am a man of few words, choosing just to observe rather than speak my mind, but it's ok, I say just enough when it counts. Like dirty talking in a woman's ear. That's when the shit counts. Or giving direction to a woman when she's sucking my dick.

After I dress, the guards cuff and shackle me, but still don't give me a guard chain. That's cool, I'm not going to go crazy again. I only save that for the people who have a need to fear the Reaper. Sounds cocky, but I know how to back it up, been backing it up all my life.

I'm escorted out of the medical building and down a path to housing A. Which is the worst of the worst, and I guess I'm considered it now. When we reach the door, we have to wait to be buzzed in, then walk to another door and get buzzed in. Making our way through that door, we happen upon a guard post with 2 guards and 3 hallways all with cells on each side. The smell of slowly dying men is overwhelming. Body odor, sweat, and defeat all permeate the air. Looking in the little windows as we walk to my cell, I can see men with their heads hanging down and some going crazy over thinking there is 'fresh meat' coming. Each cell houses two inmates, except one.

They walk me down hall C and lead me to a cell. Once inside I meet my roommate, the man I tried to get to earlier. Xavier Richards. This guy is a grade A douche bag, but I know everything about him, everyone does. The notorious gang leader who seems to be an unlikely savage. Allegedly burning men, women, and children alive if you cross him, but that is all hearsay, which means he probably has a lot of higher up contacts that keep his nose clean on paper. He's already claimed the top bunk which

I guess means I will be closest to the shitter. Fuck my life. He recognizes me instantly and bares his teeth at me like a wild animal. *Don't worry asshole, the feeling is mutual.* All we can do is stare holes through each other as the guards remove my cuffs and shackles.

The drive home is exhausting, and by the time I make it through the doors I am ready for a hot bath. But my little man awaits, wanting to hear all about my day. I swear he is going to be a guard when he grows up. He always asks me about my day, curious about the day's festivities. As soon as my feet hit the door it's 'what happened today? Anything cool go on?', and I look to my mother who is packing up her things for help with his questions, she of course just gives me that look that a mother does. That 'ha ha you were the same way when you were a kid, so you are on your own 'kind of look. With a hug and kiss to Jack and a kiss on the top of my head for me, she is out the door. She knows how he is and that there is no dissuading him from hearing all the nitty gritty details. The kid is determined, a quality he gets from me and not his sperm donor.

"Settle down, sweets, my day was boring, just new inmates," I tell him. I am certainly not going to tell him that momma feels like she is being watched, a gang banger tried coming at me, and I had to use the dick hit, or that tall, handsome, and dangerous Damian made me want to jump him. Nope, those words won't ever leave my mouth. Disappointment is evident in his walk as he goes into the living room to sit down with his little shoulders slumped.

"So what's the plan, Stan" I can see a smile being fought, but still a smile.

"Mom, nobody says that these days! You're so old!" Ouch.

"I know that, but every time I say it, it makes my baby boy smile, and you know I love that smile! That smile makes my heart melt. I made you from scratch, don't ever forget that!" I tickle his side and he cracks up which results in an all-out tickle war, plus slicing each other's butt cracks with our hands. Juvenile, yes, but you would be surprised how funny it is when someone bends over and you slice them.

"So what ya wanna do this weekend, boy?"

"Can we go to the movies to see that new fighting one?"

"Sure baby boy, now let's get rolling on dinner and a shower."

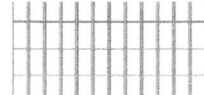

BEEP, BEEP, BEEP, BEEP. With a heavy sigh, I get on up outta my warm bed and walk into Jacks to wake him up. Kid sleeps like the dead, so I have to take all of his blankets off of him and his pillow to get him to move. One day I am gonna put his hand into some water, or attack him with a water gun. It is my civic duty as a mom to embarrass and have as much fun with my kid as I can. Seeing him rustling around lets me know he's up, and I can go start getting ready. He reminds me a lot of me, I hate waking up early, but we both hate starting our day late if we sleep in.

Thankfully, no great cereal mystery or boxer brief covered ass is greeting me when I walk into the kitchen. I think *well shit maybe he's getting it*, then I remember he's 8 and he ain't getting shit about keeping himself covered. I think that walking around in your underwear is some unwritten boy rule in life. Ingrained in them when they are young, his daddy used to do it as well. My dad, before he passed, used to always tell me when Jack was a baby that a man always comes to the table with no hat, and fully clothed. I smile to myself thinking about my dad and how much I miss him. He passed away when Jack was almost 2 from a massive stroke. I always try to make sure that Jack knows about his grand-daddy because that man was amazing.

After taking Jack to school and heading to work, I get through the gates just fine until, "Olivia, I won't open the next door if you don't go out with me, so please, put a man out of his misery and go out with me!" Josh pleads. I can't help but smile at his ruthless ways.

"When are you thinking Josh?" Since I can't see him, I stare directly at the camera knowing he can see me. "Wanna go to dinner after work?" the excitement is evident in his voice.

"Let me know where and what time and I will meet you there." Even though Josh has met Jack, he hasn't met Jack as my date. That's a whole different ball game, I don't let potential love interests into my kid's life, but shit, I need to get some sex before my vagina drops off and runs away from me. It has been way too long, and I might be a little desperate.

While I am laughing to myself because seriously my mind is way too funny, the next door buzzes open. Making my way around and into the medical building Mary tells me that I'm handling med pass and sick call in housing A and the lockdown units.

With a sigh, I load up my cart, get my gear on which is heavy and hot as hell, and make my way to block A. I reach the guards "hub" and sign in.

"Hey O, gotta wait, still shower time for a few of them, "Benton/Burton or whatever his name is tells me. He is on this block today with some guard who looks like he is about to shit himself; must be new. This prison rotates guards around the whole facility constantly, it is a safeguard that Warden Rhonda has put into place to try to combat smuggling and coercion.

I just smile and nod, it's been a while since I have been on this block. At the beginning of each cell block row is a shower, it is tiny, like can't turn around properly small, and the smell that comes from those showers is almost blinding. It's not like in those movies where it's a room full of dudes and someone drops the soap. Although the sex does happen here, it's mainly cellmates, because it's too hard to do it with anyone else when they are locked up for 23 hours a day. The yard which has the inmates that are close to going home, or not on lockdown has the communal showers. Still isn't the 'drop the soap' kind of room, it's just a row of 5 showers separated by curtains but still somewhat open.

Anyways, I have to wait. So standing there listening to Burton (that's what I am gonna go with because I think that's it, but oh well) tell the new kid how something works. I realize that he is explaining about sick call. Sick call is for the prisoners in segregation like this, seeing them at the medical center is too hard. These guys are the worst of the worst, the kind that it takes special precautions to just bring them medicine, let alone see them at the medical building. So how sick call works is, the prisoner will put a piece of paper with their request under their door. At the beginning of each shift, the guards on each corridor will collect the request the deliver them to Med Unit so we know who we are treating that day In the prison system, we have physicians that come during the day, but it's only 1 doctor and 1 dentist. So the nurses treat the inmates that are not "emergent." Unless we are stumped on something, we tell them what they will be prescribed once the next round of meds come around. We can prescribe, but the doc has to review and sign off first. Just the way it has to be with a couple thousand inmates to 1 doctor.

I feel eyes on me before I have a chance to look up and instantly my mouth goes dry and my heart begins to flutter. I look up and it's the inmate from Friday that has invaded my dreams at night, staring right at me. The man who has made me inch my fingers down my panties a few times this past weekend. The man who looks larger than life, bigger than all the other guards, is being escorted to his cell in nothing but a towel. What I wouldn't give to be that scrap of terry cloth right now. I feel my face set on fire like I am a match that was just struck. Once I look at him, I know that if he is still staring at me, that it will be written all over my face that I was just checking him out

DAMIAN

Shit! I'm standing here in a towel and sandals when I see the cute little nurse from the other day. She is swamped by a flak jacket and spit shield, but for some odd reason it looks adorably cute. She's so short that it almost looks like a little girl playing dress up. But there is no mistaking it, the only thing that makes her look little is her height, the rest of her is all woman. My dick instantly goes hard, I'm glad that I am clutching the knot in the front to keep the towel closed, it kind of hides the fact that my dick could break a rock right now. I'm stuck in this shithole with guys who are turning to other guys just to get off. No offense but no thank you. I like being able to grab a woman's tits and sink my dick into a warm, wet pussy, or slap my dick up against a woman's clit, I may not know all their names, but I remember every face that I have left satisfied. Or if I don't remember them, they certainly let me know they remember me. But this girl, ever since I first laid eyes on her this bitch hasn't left my mind, making it hard for me to concentrate on anything else.

But I see that I affect her just as much as she does me. She sees me and wears a beautiful, deep blush that creeps down her slender neck. I can't help but let that stroke my ego. She's so tiny though that I would break her in half, she wouldn't know what had hit her, and she would just fall apart into a blissful mess after I got done with her. Too bad I find myself in this situation because I would love to if given the chance. Plus it's been about a week since I got some pussy, and to me, that is a week too long. Some call me a bastard, some call me a whore, but the good thing is the bitches still call me. But now I am hard up and I'm trying to make the best of it, but I want to murder my bitch of a cell mate.

Xavier is a grade A tool, scumbag of all scumbags. Believe me when I say this, the world would be a much better place without this asshole taking up space. Even though he hasn't said shit to me, he sure talks a fucking lot. It's obvious he has done time before, because he knows the prison codes and the dirty guards. He has funneled at least 20 kites out of here just this weekend alone. Kites are nothing more than just little notes, most of the time written very small, so that they can fit more on the piece of paper. Then they are thrown out into the hall like a kite. I know he has people working for him, employees of the prison and inmates.

My attention is brought back to the moment when I hear one of the guards say, "Okay, Olivia, that was the last of the monkeys."

The guards can talk to us anyway they please, so far they have left me alone. Must be my size or the fact that I have barely grunted two words to these assholes since being here. But I can't bring myself to be mad about it because now I know a first name. Olivia, hmmm, that name is very suitable for her. I bet she even goes by Livvy or some shortened version of her name.

Making my way into my cell, I hurry up and get dressed in my prison issue scrubs that however many men before me have worn because I want to see more of her as she walks by. I wonder why she has picked a job like this because it's too dangerous for someone as pretty as she is. When you picture a prison nurse, you picture Nurse Ratched, not this cute little thing with the big brown eyes and dimples. She doesn't deserve to know the horrors that are this place. Yes, she has made it obvious that she can take care of herself, but still, it would be a fucking shame to break something so light.

"Alright, bitches med time!" That one dick guard yells out. We all knew this already with half the guys hanging in their little windows, we just want to get a look at one of the few ladies we might see while we are here. Trying not to let that thought bring the black cloud back over my head, I just think of getting my hands on her. Being able to see how responsive she really is, to see her come apart from my hands. The wheels clink and rattle unevenly against the cement floor as she pushes the cart down the corridor, breaking me from my daydream of her.

"Bitch is gonna learn don't nobody fuck with me. Gonna show her ass what the fuck is up. Stupid whore," Xavier mumbles from his bunk, his voice deep and strained. I realize then he's jerking his dick and a sick feeling of dread settles over me. He's about to fuck with her, I already know it. I can't let that happen. I know I don't take any medication, so unless he does then she will bypass us, I haven't paid attention these past couple of days because of the amount of people who stop to talk to him. Please, God, let her bypass us.

Finished playing with his one inch wonder, Xavier climbs out of his bunk and walks to the cell window. All we have is a little rectangular window facing out of our cell and a slot for food to be slipped in. He has what I can only suspect is nut in his cupped hand.

As the door opens, the guard instructs me to keep my ass on the bed. He tells Xavier something about needing some medicine for high blood pressure or some shit, but first she has to take his blood pressure. Just as I'm getting ready to say something to her, she walks right in and over to Xavier. It's like one of those moments of slow motion. I get up to stop him, and as soon as my foot hits the floor Xavier comes straight for her, and smears what is in his hand. But he didn't expect her to be wearing a riot helmet with a spit shield. So he wastes his spunk on a piece of plastic. Dumbass, serves the little piece of shit right. This only enrages him more, and it takes both guards to start pulling him away.

She jumps out of the way when he smears it on her face mask, and she kicks out and connects with his shin.

Xavier grabs his leg, bouncing on his one good foot while the guards are pulling at him to get him away.

"Stupid bitch! I'm gonna enjoy killing you slowly! Then I'm gonna go after your momma and your kid. Yeah, whore, I know all about you. Got no man to take care of you, bastard son, and it's gonna feel real good when I finally get to fuck that ass. Hell, I might make your ass watch as I kill both of them and watch as their blood is on your hands!"

She looks shaken up, her eyes glisten as tears threaten to spill over, and this odd ripping feeling in my chest takes place. Makes it hard to breathe, like a fucking elephant is sitting on me. I start rubbing between my pecs to get some relief but nothing. Is this a heart attack? I don't know what's wrong, inside I am panicking but hoping on the outside I don't look like shit is bothering me. If I drop dead right here, then all of this shit will be for nothing.

Olivia

Holy shit! That fucker just smeared cum on me. Well, my helmet but fuck it's been a while since we have had someone go after us, and this makes it twice now that this particular inmate has come after *me*. This guy scares me and when I hear his words, a chill runs up and down my spine because I know if given the opportunity, he would follow through. I'm terrified but trying not to let it show. The fear is gripping me, my spine feels like it is frozen solid with the chills having gone up and down them. Funny how my back is cold but in this mask I have sweat dripping into my eyes. I would give anything to take it off, but I can't with his spunk on the front mask. So I just school my features while my insides go to war between hot and cold.

Burton and the new guard didn't do shit except try to restrain Xavier. The only one that looks affected in all of this is his cell mate. Now that I've had a better look I see it's Damian. This time, he has his prison- issued scrub pants on. Fuck him too, fuck all four of them.

Excusing myself, I leave the cell and walk down the block to the guard station to clean my mask. I pull on some clean gloves. I still have a job to do, so after drying my mask and washing my hands I head back to their cell. Burton tells the new guard to cuff Damian so that he is restrained while Burton lays Xavier down on what I assume is Damian's bed. They have since hog tied him while I was cleaning my mask. I finally get his blood pressure and then hand the guards the meds. Other than the occasional insulin or bp check, we don't give the inmates their meds directly, we hand off to the guard, who in turn hands them to the inmate.

After the catastrophe that was med pass is done, I finally make it back to the clinic. Josh is standing there waiting for me. Great, just what I need, him fussing over me.

"I just fucking heard, are you ok?" He yells as he looks me over. The feeling I have with Josh is not like the feeling I have with that fuckwad in building A. Where Damian is all fire, Josh is like seeing an ex-boyfriend that you have stayed friends with. No feelings except you hope they have a good day. I guess this doesn't bode well for Josh or my vagina. I assure him that I'm fine and that yes, after changing and showering, we will still go to dinner tonight.

Leaving work is a big ole mess, because I have to fill out an incident report over the Xavier incident, which puts me late getting home. Our prison has their own police force that will investigate and report to the warden. I've met the warden a few times, she's a nice lady, but I hear that once you cross Rhonda you will wish you were dead. She certainly has the capabilities to make your life hell. I guess being a woman in her high profile position means she has to be that way to survive it. So I keep my head down and my nose clean, she has no reason to talk to me, and I don't have one to return the favor.

Jack wondered why I was so late and why Grandma was hanging around. I told him that I was going out with a friend for dinner, and I would be back to tuck him into bed.

"Who is the friend, Mom?" A strange look passes over his face. Not a look of curiosity but seems like a look of longing.

"A friend from work, why ya asking kiddo?"

"A boy or girl? Where ya going? Do I know them?"

"It's Josh, and we are just going to dinner. You remember Josh right?"

He nods, but the look of longing has kind of transformed. Could it be that Jack is craving to have a man in his life too? I file that away to talk to Mom about later. For now I gotta scoot so I'm not late. I am not a late kind of person, I would rather be way early than on time, and to be late? Being late to me is tantamount to lying. Of course things happen that are unforeseeable, but if you tell me you will be somewhere at a certain time, be there at that time or you're lying.

Dinner with Josh is rather uneventful, it's like going out with a friend. No spark, no chemistry, just a peck on the cheek before I get in my car. He looks a little wounded, but promises that he's ok. I consider Josh a friend, and I don't want to hurt his feelings, but I just don't see this going anywhere. I want passion and fire, and with Josh it just feels like eating vanilla ice cream with nothing else forever.

Jack's playing video games when I get home, his hair still damp from his shower. So I just sit next to him and watch, thinking back of when he was an itty bitty and I held him so tight in my arms. Makes me wish I had another baby, but that lack of a man makes it impossible. One day, maybe. I'm still young, and I think Jack would be ok with a baby brother or sister to play with.

"Stop staring at me, Momma, it's rude!"

"Not staring, just looking at you and how handsome you have become. Do you ever wish you had a brother or sister?" I ask cautiously.

"Nope, I like it being just us. Wish sometimes I had someone to play catch with because, Mom, you throw like a girl, and I call you butter fingers." Well ok then. There goes my NFL dreams.

Shortly after, I settle Jack into bed, kiss his little head and leave his room thinking about what he said. I wish I could find a man that would play catch with him and teach him all the boy things that he needs to know. Mom and I try, but I know how hard it is for him. I feel the same way too, I want him to have those things. I want someone for me, so I don't go to bed lonely every night. These are the small times when I miss Jack's dad, but I know deep down that we are better off without him. Unfortunately nobody has come into our lives that I have deemed worthy of being a dad to my son.

Getting up for work in the morning, I let out a huge sigh. I spent all night last night tossing and turning, replaying what Jack said and staring down a pair of blue eyes. I can't seem to get Damian out of my mind, I mean seriously? Why am I lusting after an inmate? I can't believe I didn't look at what he did, or as all the other inmates tell me "allegedly" did. Normally I look right off the bat, because hello, I gotta protect myself. I can only chalk it up to his hypnotizing eyes and the earlier drama with Xavier. I make a mental note to pull up his file from our computer system and look up what he did and how much time he has to serve. Then once I see maybe that will curb my attraction to him. Don't get me wrong, there are guys who are cute or hot that come to prison. Then you look at what heinous things they did and all cuteness goes out the window.

DAMIAN

I lie awake at night thinking about her. She invades my dreams, but it's almost like a nightmare. I have nowhere to turn because she is always there. A nightmare because I cannot touch her. A nightmare because I know that I can never have her. After watching in horror at what Xavier did, I noticed that even though she had a face shield smeared in cum, she never cried, she looked a little shaken up. When she came back from cleaning up she showed zero emotion, she must be used to it, even though that's incredibly disturbing. These guys take any chance that they can to act out or to show their asses for the few ladies that they see.

Thankfully Xavier has been in solitary confinement since he fucked up, and I couldn't be happier about it. Not smelling his shit and being able to jerk my dick whenever I want has made me a happy guy. I can't believe it has been over a week since I have been balls deep in a woman.

Never knew I could go so long, thought my dick might fall off if I did. Now all I have is my thoughts of this tiny pixie of a woman and my hands to take care of business. My hands and my dick have been meeting daily over that woman. My current circumstance may get in the way, but, my dick knows that I want her. My dick doesn't care that I am locked in a cell for 23 hours a day, or that I have to be cuffed and shackled wherever I go. No, my dick is like a heat seeking missile straight to Olivia.

I've never had a problem getting women, and I certainly never have a problem getting a woman off. I take pride in my abilities to use my fingers, tongue, and dick. Normally I have a woman begging for more.

Conceited?

Sure, but I know how good I am and I can back up that fact. One day I hope to get my hands on her cute little heart shaped ass and show her that I am not just some criminal.

"Xavier is coming back today," I hear one inmate call to another. Fan-fucking-tastic. I hate this bitch. He's a piece of shit leader in the Devils, which is a local gang around here. It's gotten bigger over the years and Xavier is the reason why. For whatever reason, he can run a gang. They recruit young kids and set them up for a life of crime. Xavier is a part of the scum of the earth. He would shoot your momma if you owe him money or invading on his "district." He is accused of participating or ordering hundreds of different crimes. One day the fucker will slip up and then his ass will be on death row.

I want to just yell out 'fuck him,' but I know that will turn the heat on me, and I can't afford heat on me with him being my cell mate. If the secrets I'm harboring came to life in this shit hole, it would put a lot of people in danger, not to mention get me killed. Besides, I don't think his punk ass is going to give up on tormenting Olivia. Just thinking her name has me hard as a rock, so much so that I could probably use the tip of my dick as a hammer. So it's safer for all those around me whether directly or indirectly like Olivia if I play by the rules and keep my mouth shut.

"Inmate Shaw, up and at it," a guard shouts into my window.

"The fuck you want?" Never biting my tongue when talking to a guard, never have and certainly never will. They may get to talk to us like we are trash, but I certainly will give it back to them. Bastards. Just like any profession there are good and bad. Sadly in the guard world, the bad outweighs the good. Most of them will smuggle cigarettes in their anus for the right price. Don't get me started on how easy it is to bribe a guard.

"Warden wants to see you in her office, gotta get shackled."

I know what this is about, doesn't make me want to go and sit there and listen to her bitch. I have nothing to say to her. She's going to ream me up one side and down the other. She knows my secrets, she's the only one who does, though. So I have no choice but to sit and take her lecture.

Olivia

Beep, Beep, Beep.

Ugh, Tuesday, its dark and gloomy out like the sky is about to open up and rain down on us, and wash us all away. I kind of hope it does, even though I have to work. I love a good thunderstorm. Something about the crack of thunder that has a way of soothing the soul, like the rumble you feel is rumbling the bad right out of you. At least to me it is, but today I hope goes well. I hope that nothing happens and most of all, I hope my med pass is in the yard. Cori can take care of the blocks, she usually does most days.

Teddy is at the gate when I first arrive, and it's nice to see his face again. I have no idea why he has been out, but I haven't seen him lately. After buzzing me back, I realize there is a new guard manning the metal detector. I guess they go through a lot of guards sometimes. Some people think they are tough enough and some are. But some fizzle out a few days after starting, running away with their tails between their legs. Same with the nurses here. We have 2 nurses on night shift, but during the day it's Mary, Cori and myself. We have a few labor pool ones that we can call in if need be like Ryan and all his smarminess, but that's a rarity. So we have a good system going with the few doctors and us nurses. It works for us because we know what Mary expects, we know how she operates her clinic and we know her rules. I often wonder to myself how this place would function without her here. She seems to be a backbone to this prison and definitely to the medical clinic. She seems to sense what the docs need before they can even voice it.

Walking into the clinic, Mary is stocking supplies, and I can hear her grumbling to herself. This does not bode well for the day. Whenever Mary gets in one of those moods we know to watch out, so we don't feel the wrath of her attitude. I have worked here long enough and seen her chew out enough people that I know to steer clear. I try to duck into the med room and Cori is filling meds.

"Sup, bitch?" She is so brash, but I love her all the same. Couldn't ask for a better friend. She is taller than me by a couple inches and has this long blonde hair with the underneath dyed black. She wears it in a bun when working, but wraps the black underside all around the bun. Makes her look like Cruella.

"Nada, whore, saw Mary and ran!"

"Yeah, she's been talking to herself for a while now, she assigned me to the yard today."

"Ugh, Cori, can you please switch with me?" I'm whining I know, but I cannot stand to go back and see Damian or Xavier.

"Nope, Mary said I had to do yard for the next few weeks, you got cells, sorry!" and she has the nerve to look sad about it. We both hate doing the cell blocks and often fight over who will do it.

With a heavy weighted feeling in my legs, like the Mafia is wanting my ass to 'sleep with the fishes' I gather all of my supplies and head off to A block. After signing in, I notice both of the guards do not look familiar, must be that staffing change time of year.

It never ceases to amaze me how the inmates can see from those little rectangle windows. I feel his eyes on me instantly, and it's a gentle caress that comforts me. An unspoken promise that he is looking out for me. His eyes cloak me in a protective shield, and when he's looking at me I feel safe. Even though it was evident the other day that he wasn't. I wish that were the case, not just because of Xavier, but because life happens and having a big hulking man would make life happen a little easier. Ugh, listen to me, lusting after a damn inmate! If it were some other girl and she told me about this same predicament, I would laugh at her then buy her a gigolo. I mentally remind myself to buy some batteries for my standby boyfriend B.O.B. He never cheats, lies or lets me down.

Making my way to Damian's cell, I see that Xavier is back from solitary confinement. Fantastic. Just what I wanted, hopefully, he keeps his spunk to himself this time. Unfortunately with the flak jacket, I can't reach my dick hitter. Not having it makes me feel uneasy, I am putting all of my trust into a thick jacket and a plastic shield. Being able to reach my hitter would make me feel ten times better when dealing with this creep.

"Bitch came back for more huh, D?" Xavier hops down from his top bunk. Damian just stares back at him. I guess these creeps are friends, figures. Assholes always flock together and it never seems to fail. Olivia always finding the wrong guys hot, guess it's the bad boy complex. *We all want a bad boy, just not to have to fix a bad boy.*

You can hear crickets chirp from Damian, and Xavier just doesn't care. I think he likes the sound of his own voice too much. To me, it sounds like nails on a chalkboard, it gives the feeling of a snake slithering in the grass. At any time that snake could strike and you would be done.

"Shut up, Richards," the guard yells at him as we step inside of their cell.

"Fuck you, rent-a-pig. This whore will know soon enough who she fucked with, and then she won't be escaping me. Wonder how those big brownies will look with no life in them."

We get threatened all the time by stupid ass inmates who don't realize that their words don't scare me. Most of the time they back off as they serve their time, often becoming very friendly towards us. Most of them are just angry at their circumstances. Xavier, however, seems to not want to give up.

I finish checking his bp and giving him his meds. I don't know if I can deal with the next few weeks of having to see him 5 days a week. He seems relentless, and who the hell wants to deal with that?

Quickly I finish up with all the corridors of housing A, but it's when I get to housing B that sends a chill up my spine. Apparently Xavier has a further reach than I realized. Hushed whispers fill the corridor as I approach the inmate cells. I can't make out clearly what's being said, but they all have my name hanging from their lips.

"You don't know who you fucked with, bitch! You gonna get yours. X don't leave no witnesses neither, so y'all best better run while you still got a chance. Last I heard, the last girl that dissed him, her family got mailed pieces of her and her kids." He is usually a nice guy, always calling me Miss Olivia. But today, it is almost as if a switch has been flipped and the look of pure hatred in his eyes stops me on a dime. He must be a part of the Devils.

An ominous feeling comes over me and I feel like whatever it will be, will be ginormous. Making my way back to the clinic, I can't help but start to panic inside. I'm hoping that panic does not show on my face until I figure out what is going to come of this. These guys feed off of the emotions of others. So if I am showing the panic on my face, these guys would feed off of it. My number one priority in all of this is Jack and his safety. If something were to happen to him, I would go insane. Just the thought terrifies me down to my core.

Cori is in the clinic by the time I make it back from my rounds and sends me a megawatt smile. Little does she know that my stomach feels like it is going to fall out my ass!

"You look like dog shit, run over!" Great. I thought I had the RBF in place, but I guess not.

"I think I am just hungry. Hopefully I will feel better after lunch."

"I am getting the food here, you wanna come?"

"Yeah, I ran out the door without bringing mine."

Making our way to the cafeteria, I say a silent prayer that whatever guards are on kitchen duty are actually paying attention to the inmates as they prepare the food. You read about these horror stories of inmates putting all kinds of shit in food. But fortunately, that rumor hasn't gone around here. Warden Rhonda always makes it a point to eat the food here, and I figure if she is still around, then they aren't doing anything wrong. Besides, I'm definitely small fish compared to her.

Getting our whatever the hell this shit is, we carry our stuff to a table. There are yard inmates all around, but I have known these guys for some months now. I would never trust any of them, but I can eat without worry around them, especially in this cafeteria with 6 guards watching everything, plus guards in the kitchen. I still feel like the bottom of my world will drop out, but I am hoping that nobody can see the hell I am living through right now. I am pretty sure that if I went to Mary with my concerns she would send me to talk to the warden. That would be like signing my death warrant because people talk in this place. Not blaming the warden, I am sure she would try to keep it hush hush, but I am not taking that chance.

Once Cori and I make it back to the clinic from lunch, Mary tells me I need to head on over to the housing units because I am handling sick call. I instantly cringe on the inside. I hope that Xavier hasn't put a slip in to be seen. I can say that I am excited at the possibility of seeing Damian again. Sick call sucks, because you are crammed in a tiny, smelly ass room the size of a pantry, with the inmate. The guard is with us, but there is a line of other inmates waiting. So it can be very dangerous because it's you and a guard against 10-15 other inmates. Last year, we had a nurse get her nose broken during sick call because of an inmate going crazy on her and the guard. Well, he tried fighting the guard, she just took an elbow to the face because of the size of the room.

DAMIAN

I notice Xavier passes notes with the guards often. He's plotting something, and I feel it in my bones. He is targeting Olivia, but it seems more than that. The atmosphere in this block has changed, it's almost tangible. Like we are all waiting to go to slaughter in a slaughterhouse. I send over a slip for sick call in the hopes that I can get Olivia to see me, let alone put her hands on me. I don't even have anything wrong with me. How sick is that? I used to be this big badass, fuck a different woman every day of the week. But here I am hoping that she will be working sick call just so I can see her. I think I would come in my pants if she were to touch me, hell, my dick might leap outta my pants. Plus maybe I can warn her, don't know of what, but I feel like she needs some kind of protection.

The guards line us up in the corridor to wait for sick call. There are 3 guards on shift at all times monitoring our moves while in transport through the prison with cattle prods and riot shields. More so for their own protection because there are some crazy son of a bitches behind the gate. They're all on high alert, a thick tension swirling about the air.

I line up with Xavier right in front of me. It's a good thing he's in front of me to be seen because then I can somewhat hear what's going on in the patient room. I know she has a guard in there with her, but I don't trust none of these motherfuckers.

Xavier is here for the same reason as I am, Olivia. Although our agendas are very different. He wants to hurt her, I want to fuck her up against the wall. I want to bury my dick to the hilt in her wet heat. I think she would be a screamer as she clenches my dick like a vise. He, on the other hand, wants to see her die. He is one crazy motherfucker, and I'm keeping my eyes on every single minute of the day. I'm like his shadow, even though he doesn't know it. He just thinks I'm some slow idiot because I don't speak much. I don't need to, actions speak louder and all that bullshit.

As we are waiting our turn he calls the guard over, I think his name is Burton. They whisper something back and forth to each other and like a dog my hackles go up. Something isn't sitting right with me. My gut is screaming at me that he's a dirty guard, I can feel it burn like fire all the way down to my toes, but I don't have solid proof of anything yet.

I am trying to gauge the situation without giving myself away. If I draw suspicion to myself, then I won't be able to get closer to Xavier. His waste of space ass is nothing but a chatterbox, all he does is yammer all the time. About the men he's killed, the women he raped, and the children he has tortured. He is the epitome of evil, and I want nothing more than to kill him myself and celebrate in his blood. The state should give me an award for taking him out. But I am getting closer to him. I have a whole list of evil deeds he has said out loud, and suspicions of the ones he hasn't said much about.

Standing here, I'm wondering what the fuck they are talking about, and I wish at this moment I knew how the fuck to read lips. I see them pound knuckles, but Xavier has a shit eating grin on his face. Xavier is up next, and sweat fucking beads across my brow as my anxiety grows.

If he does something to her, I will kill him with my bare hands.

As the last inmate is escorted out of the patient room, Burton guides Xavier inside, closing the door behind them.

4 walls.

1 door.

2 vicious and vile bastards.

1 cute little pixie with no means of escape.

I can't help but crowd right by the door, waiting to hear any screams. Even handcuffed I will break this fucking door down.

"Bitch." Xavier says, but I can't make out the rest. He's not shouting so I am assuming that's a good thing. I don't hear any screaming or any rustling of anything, so I am hoping she is safe for now. I hope I can keep her alive for good, but the only way to do that is to stop this Xavier motherfucker.

Olivia

Xavier gives me the creeps. He so far has tried to back me into a corner, but I stood my ground. He's here because he's having 'headaches,' stupid fucker even does the air quotes when he tells me about them. It takes everything in me not to laugh in his face, but I'm afraid of what he would do if I did. All I can think of is protecting Jack. He needs me and if I get myself killed by some wannabe thug, then he will have only my mom, and she isn't exactly a spring chicken.

"There is really nothing I can do for you about a headache," I tell him and he instantly looks disgusted. Like he smells shit.

"Whatever, bitch, I just wanted to get your smell one last time." Fuck. He definitely knows how to rattle me to my bones.

"I can send some Aspirin to you on the next med distribution."

"Keep it, the smell of your fear is enough to cure a headache." He even sniffs the air as if he can actually smell my fear.

He looks to the guard, Burton, and together they walk out. Before I can even get to the door, Damian is barging in. I have to keep telling myself to keep it cool, he's an inmate, and I should not be relieved or happy to see him. But I am.

Standing in front of me he has this look in his eyes, almost feral like a lion stalking his prey. I should be scared, I know that, but I'm not.

"The fuck did he do?" He growls, literally growls at me!

"Huh?" I'm confused, who is he talking about? These are the first words he has spoken to me on his own, without me asking a question first.

"What. The. Fuck. Did. He. Do?" he says slower like I am a young child not quite getting the question.

"N-n-nothing," I stammer out, having to look up because shit he is tall and scrumptious. My mouth suddenly feels dry.

"Don't fucking lie to me, what the fuck did he do to you?"

"Look, he really didn't do anything, do you think Burton would let that happen?" It's then I realize, there is no guard in here with us. We will be in deep shit unless we get down to business.

"You would be surprised what that sick fuck could do, do you honestly think you are safe even with the guards?"

He's still crowding in my space but I admit, I really like it. He has a strong presence, the kind that if he goes to speak, you listen, and those baby blues do not hurt matters. I wonder why there is no guard here. That scares me, like down to my toes. His words *'Do you really think you are safe even with guards'* play in my mind. I guess I have always trusted people on face value.

Once I gather my composure and put on the RBF, I ask him what he's being seen for today. Him answering, 'you', is not what I expected. My cheeks heat, I have to clench my thighs together to keep myself from moaning, because yes, please. I really want him to want me. He seems unaffected by my presence, so obviously he doesn't intend to lay me down and screw me. Jesus, I need to get laid, because whenever I look at this man all I can think about is sex. I need to dust out the cobwebs, because obviously if I am getting horny talking to an inmate then B.O.B. isn't doing the job.

DAMIAN

I barely give Xavier and the guard time to leave the room before I barge in to check on Olivia. I could tell he did something because she has a slight tremble to her, and she is paler than her normal porcelain skin. What he did, I don't know, she won't say and that pisses me off to no end. But I did make her blush, which, by the way, is the most incredibly beautiful thing I have ever seen. My ego soars because I was beginning to feel like I was slowly losing my touch along with my sanity being locked up in this shithole. I want to reach out and touch her, but she looks like a scared kitten waiting to swat in defense, so I don't think she would want to be comforted by the likes of someone like me.

When she asks what I am being seen for, I can definitely tell she wasn't expecting my response, and the blush that I receive in return causes my dick to stir. I feel like I could pound nails with my cock right now. Shower time is going to be another night of taking care of business so my balls don't explode. I want her and it's quickly turning into needing her, or better yet, needing a reaction out of her. But I don't know her, and I have no idea why I feel this way.

At this time a guard walks in, Josh I think is his name. Seems like an ok guy, but he stares at her a little too long for my liking.

"What the hell is going on in here? Olivia, you know that you cannot be around an inmate without a guard! Are you trying to get your ass fired?" He is downright angry now. Don't blame him, but I can't help but growl at him. He ain't talking to her that way.

"Josh, as you can see I'm fine." She looks ashamed that she was caught with me. I don't blame her. I'm an inmate, I've done bad things in life, and I am sure that I will do more bad things when given the chance. Whether it be love them and leave them with many women, or beating someone to a pulp, she still shouldn't be around me alone.

"Don't let it happen again! You're lucky he's not a murderer!" he yells out at us. I don't understand what his deal is. He has a look of lust I his eyes that's a little too wild for me, almost like he is obsessed with her. He must want to fuck her, but I bet not as much as me. Being in prison teaches you how to read people. Helps you avoid fights when you are in general population.

"I'm sorry," she mutters quietly.

As soon as she says the words I'm instantly pissed. Who does this pansy ass wanna be cop think he is? She has nothing to apologize for. If he wants to come down on someone, it should be me.

"Sweetheart, you don't have to apologize," I say looking into her eyes. It's like the douchebag has faded away and its only me and her in the room. I see the blush creep up her neck again, and I feel like I have just won the Olympics. It's a feeling that rushes straight through from the top of my head to the tips of my toes.

"The fuck are you doing Olivia? Do you know this creep?" he roars at us.

"Josh, no, I don't know him and you are not my boyfriend, I don't know what more you want me to say. I apologized, so let's drop it." And just like that, my dick is hard again. This little pixie of a girl has some fire and chops.

A knock at the door stops all three of us. It's Burton, I guess ready to take me back to my cell. Olivia backs away from both Burton and Dick Head Josh. I give one last look at her, wink and walk towards the door. I'm ready to go because the tension in the room is palpable almost like something that you could taste…pungent and powerful.

Olivia

What the hell just happened? I mean I am so confused, and now I have Josh looking at me like he wants to wring my neck, Burton glowering like always it seems and Damian just strutting away. It's a damn fine strut, too. But that's besides the point! One minute he is being this sweet man concerned for my safety, the next with Josh here, he seems like a dick.

"Olivia, seriously, are you trying to lose your job?" Josh asks me with judgment written all over him. It's kind of like we can all tell when someone is judging us, they look at you like you smell like shit. Oh well, I guess this is really just true colors coming through. I thought Josh was a nice guy, but I can see now that it's probably not the case. The look on his face right now reminds me of one my mother would give me when I was a kid and did something wrong.

"Josh, I am not trying to lose my job, he came in before I could stop him. But if you think you can come in and boss me around, then you got another thing coming. Because I am not your woman, nor will I ever be, and you are not my boss!"

"Fine, Olivia. But I'll be standing guard in the room while Burton escorts the inmates in and out, just to play it safe." Cocky bastard backs into the corner glowering at me.

I breeze through the rest of the inmates that are in line. Most are diabetics that need their feet checked, or have simple ailments, like athlete's foot and jock itch. Nothing that requires any of them to come back to the clinic. Josh gives me one last look of disgust and books it out of there with a quickness. Oh well, if he is going to treat me that way after one date, he certainly isn't the candidate I want to dust the cobwebs off. No love lost between me and him.

Thankfully the rest of my day flies by and there no more run-ins with Xavier or Josh. Sadly that means no more running into Damian. I can say that I am actually sad about that. Something about that man both turns me on and scares me. His eyes are so intense like he is not just looking at your outer shell, but straight into your heart and soul. Never before have I experienced it. It's terrifying because you feel as if you can hide no secrets, he knows them all.

Jack is waiting on me when I get home, practically bouncing up and down to tell me that he has learned how to ride a bike without training wheels. I jump up and down with him because that's amazing. I have tried and tried to show him, but he just wasn't getting the hang of it. Sad that I didn't get to see the first time, but it's still awesome.

"Go get your helmet on, I want to watch you ride around the yard." And like a flash of movement out the corner of my eye, he is gone and getting his helmet.

"I'm so ready, I can't believe I did it, Mom!"

"I always knew you could. Told you, you just had to believe that you could and straighten up that leg."

I sit on the front porch and watch him ride his bike proudly. I feel my cell phone buzz in my pocket. Hmmm, that's odd, I don't know this number. Ignore city then. Nobody has time for a wrong number these days, let alone a telemarketer. Brushing it off as nothing, I watch Jack as he makes it quite a few feet then just stopping all by himself. He is growing up so fast, that I don't know what I will do when he is an adult. It's always been just me and him. The thought of him older and possibly off at college has me wishing I could hold him and that will stop him from growing up.

After dinner, homework, and a shower, we snuggle up on the couch and watch some TV. Jack is a huge wrestling fan so we always end up watching that. His face lights up in pure awe and excitement as he watches one of his favorite high flyers jump from the top of the ring, and it gives me joy to see my boy so captivated.

"Mom, help me, I'm sick!" I hear being yelled from the bathroom at 2 am.

"Coming baby."

Rushing into the bathroom the poor boy is clutching the toilet like it's a lifeline. He looks green around the gills and seems to have thrown up yesterday's dinner. I'm exhausted but immediately jump into momma nurse mode. I get him a cold washcloth to put on his neck then go ready a trash can with a bag inside and bring him to my bed. After some medicine and watching some more wrestling in bed, he is safely asleep in my arms, running a fever. With a sigh, I text Mary to call off sick.

We spend the day in bed eating soup and watching movies. He is such a nut for action movies. I'd never tell him, but those are my favorites too. I like having him watch chick flicks with me because it helps me teach him how to be a man and how a man should act. By the end of the day Jack is feeling better, puke and fever free. So thankfully he's going to school tomorrow, and I can make it to work.

Mary called earlier to tell me that since I was out today, I needed to cover on Saturday. My cell rings, and not even looking at the number I pick up so not to disturb Jack who is sleeping peacefully.

"Hello."

"You're gonna die, bitch." Xavier's voice pierces the line, sounding like sandpaper on wood. It's a unique sound, rough and edgy. You don't doubt that his words carry the weight of what he means.

"Who is this?" I ask, my insides are screaming at me in a panic, so it is making me doubt that it is even him on the phone.

"The last person that will see you alive. I can't wait to taste your blood on my lips. Can't wait to hear your screams and watch you beg for me to end your suffering." A sinister laugh fills the call before he hangs up.

I look at the caller i.d. and it's a private caller. I quickly run through my house and check all windows and door. I call my cell company to get details of where the call came from and they tell me that it was made from a payphone. I call the police and they take a report, but there is nothing they can do since it was from a payphone. Who knew payphones were still around because I surely didn't? I know logically in my head that there are payphones at the prison, I also know logically that it was Xavier, but it's like my head won't wrap around the truth. Luckily Jack didn't wake up through any of this or he would be freaking out. Hell, I'm freaking out! Sleep doesn't come easy for me, I toss and turn all night until the alarm goes off in the morning.

Dropping Jack at school I can tell he knows something is up. He was quiet on the whole ride, and I seem to be snapping more than usual at him. He couldn't wait to jump out of the car and run into school by the time we made it there. I keep a close eye watching my mirrors in case anyone is following me, and I was too scared to stop somewhere that I didn't even stop for my morning soda.

Walking towards the clinic I hear, "Olivia, can I talk to you for a second?" Shit! It's Rhonda, the prison Warden. *Of course you can talk to me, you're basically my boss* is the words running through my head. We walk into the clinic, and I get the key from Cori to the med room. Seems like this is as private of a place to go to talk. Cori's eyes get big when she sees who is standing behind me.

"Olivia, it has come to my attention that you were alone with an inmate in the exam room in housing A two days ago, care to explain why? Because I am sure that you know that fraternizing with an inmate is grounds for dismissal." The way this lady carries herself scares me, she is very no nonsense. I wonder if she has any friends.

"Well, I had just gotten done with inmate Xavier Richards' exam, he was being escorted back to his cell, when inmate Damian Shaw came in. It wasn't intentional on my part to not have a guard, and inmate Shaw is new and might not have known protocol."

"Did Shaw threaten you?"

"Not in any way, ma'am."

"You do realize how important it is to have a guard with you at all times, you know that you could lose your job for this, but seeing as how we have never had any kind of issue with you, we will let it slide this time. With a warning, of course. Next time you won't be so fortunate. I expect that you have a guard at any and every time you are in the blocks. It would be a shame to lose you, Olivia, but you are easily replaceable."

With that, she walks out. I'm flabbergasted because I have never had any kind of disciplinary problems in the time that I have worked here, so I'm surprised that my first time came from Rhonda herself. I would have assumed Mary would have handled that. That lady is scary, and with the rumors that have gone around about her, she can handle her own in every situation.

Now that my stomach has stopped trying to drop out of my butt, I am pissed. Josh had to have done this, the douchebag. I want to kick his balls up in his throat, but then I know I would really get fired. Putting the bitchface into place, I get set up for the day. Determined not to let Rhonda, Josh, or Xavier get me down.

"What did she want?" Cori is practically squealing in excitement just knowing she might hear some gossip. I expect the foaming at the mouth to happen soon because this girl is ravenous for some juicy details. Gossip rarely happens in the clinic, so both she and I love to hear it whenever we can.

"Nothing really, she just warned me because of the issue with Shaw during sick call the other day." Cori already knew about the Damian incident because we text constantly when we aren't at work.

"Boo," she says as if she is truly disappointed with the gossip.

"Sorry bitch, next time it will be juicier," sarcasm drips from my retort. She slaps my ass and walks away. She really is my other half in this crazy world. Cori is the type of girl that people gravitate towards because she is so friendly and bubbly. I, on the other hand, am not bubbly, so she brings it out in me.

Walking into housing A, I get the butterflies in my belly and I know why. Damian. He has starred in more than one of my dreams at night; the tattoos, the eyes, just everything about him is so mouthwatering that a girl can't help but to dream of him. I see that Burton is one of the guards today. Great, he's a tool, but I can't pick what guards are going to be where. Certainly is a step up from Josh, though. Just thinking about him has me seething. He is apparently paranoid about where he stands with me. Little does he know he stands nowhere near me and didn't even before he tattled on me. He has just cemented that position because apparently he is a 2-year-old who tattles to their Moms.

Walking down the corridor with Burton I notice that it's silent. No inmates are talking which sends shivers down my spine. I instantly go on high alert because something is wrong, there is almost a crackle of electricity in the air. Making our way to Xavier and Damian's cell, Burton starts opening the door.

"What the fuck is this!" I hear him yell out, but before I can look up from grabbing my blood pressure cuff and Xavier's meds, I see a flash of orange flicker in my peripheral and feel the most incredible heat I have ever felt. A blood-curdling scream echoes through the small cell and I look up to see that Burton is set up in flames, thrashing around violently. The smell, the smell is just overwhelming. I freeze in a panic, rooted to where I stand for a few seconds before I can jump into action. Nothing this heinous has ever happened at this prison. Oh my God! Doing the only thing I can, I shove my way into the room and push Burton down on the ground and out into the hallway, trying to get him to stop, drop and roll. But I know it's too late. His movement has stilled as the flames settle, a thick, pungent smoke billowing from his body. I press my fingers to his charred skin to confirm what I already know and pieces of flesh come back on my fingers. Just as I reach for his radio to call for help, I see someone tower over me, and I know… I just know that this is the end.

DAMIAN

Holy Shit! That crazy motherfucker just lit that guard on fire. I think he was hoping it was Olivia, I didn't even see him with anything. I've been watching this crazy bitch for days now and nothing. Looking over at him, he is smiling this cruel smile. He looks like a dog stalking his prey, just pure viciousness. I am waiting to hear the other guards, but I don't know where they went to. They had to have heard this, hell the screams the guy let out should have been heard prison-wide. I guess Xavier has more guards on his payroll than I thought because someone should be here by now. The other inmates are going wild in their cells making it hard to hear anything. Olivia is down on the floor over the guard. I know he's gone, but she is trying hard to save him. Xavier stalks towards her, but I react on instinct and charge into the cell hitting that motherfucker in the back, crashing his head against the concrete wall. I grab Olivia by the arm and haul her to the guard's room at the end of the hall, locking us in. I don't think she realizes it's me because she is thrashing about, kicking and clawing at me. But then again to her I am an inmate, so she has every reason to be scared.

I force her down in a chair, she's starting to panic, and I don't have time for this right now. Looking out the window I can see that Xavier has the dead guard's keys and is opening the cells to the other inmates. This is going to be a full on prison break. I have to get us out of here. Pandemonium is breaking out as inmates are released from their cells. They run through the corridor, screaming and shouting. A few have even gone over to the guard and are pissing on him and kicking at his lifeless form. It is doing nothing to help the smell of burnt flesh.

"Olivia, is there some button to push for this, like a panic button or riot button or something?" I would assume prisons would have a panic button that would alert others of trouble, but I guess not.

"H-h-huh?" Great. I don't have time for a panic attack. I know she's scared, but we have to move if I am going to save our lives.

"Baby, look at me" I am trying to be soothing, but she's frozen in place completely consumed with panic.

"Bitch LOOK AT ME!" I roar in her face hoping to startle her into getting her head in the game. Even though trembling and covered in someone else's gore, she is the most beautiful thing I have ever seen. But now is not the time for that as Xavier is getting closer with a group of inmates and we are sitting ducks in here.

Finally, I see her eyes. "There you are, ok, is there a protocol or a button or something to alert the other guards and shit that these motherfuckers are making a jailbreak?"

"I don't know, I'm not a guard!" She grabs the phone and dials a set numbers. 'Um, yes, this is Olivia Conway, and I'm at housing A and the inmates are free, there is a guard dead, please send help.' With a shaky hand, she sets the receiver down. I know that the info has been received because all of a sudden there is a loud alarm. Looking down at her, she is rocking back and forth hugging her arms to her chest. I can't deal with that right now, Xavier is still freeing inmates and will be to us in a second, the other inmates are already beating on the windows. The windows are bulletproof, but they won't hold forever.

The emergency exit door at the other end of the hallways is already open and some inmates are spilling out of that into other parts of the prison. Shit this is a clusterfuck. I've been watching Xavier for a while now so I know how far his criminal reach is. He is ruthless and will stop at nothing. I need a plan.

Olivia

Burton is dead. It's all I keep repeating to myself as I sit here rocking back and forth. I'm terrified and have no idea how I am going to get through this. Jack. My sweet baby Jack. I am going to fight until I can't fight anymore to get home to my baby boy. He needs me, things can't end this way. I can't flipping die in a dingy ass prison, not telling my son I love him one last time. Now I am locked in the guards' room with an inmate all the while chaos ensues through the block. I don't know what the fuck to do.

Damian seems like he is going to protect me, but I don't know him. He's Xavier's cell mate so maybe this is a plot to get me alone. But then again he had me call it in, so maybe they aren't working together. I'm so confused about what to do, what is going on, how I can stay alive in this situation. Slowly I start backing away from him.

He seems lost in thought, probably wondering how the hell he is going to get out of here.

"Don't back away from me. I know what you're thinking, it's written all over your face, Livvy. I had nothing to do with this shit. I would never put you in danger. You have to believe me that things aren't always what they seem."

"Don't call me Livvy!" My ex used to call me Livvy when he did something wrong, it was his tell. Since he split that nickname grates on my last nerve. I refuse to let anyone call me that name again. Especially some inmate.

"Ok, Olivia, again, I had nothing to do with this. I promise you that, and I promise to not hurt you. But we need to get out of here. We can't sit in this room because he is steadily releasing people from their cells and soon he can overpower this room. Bulletproof glass only lasts so long."

I know he's right, but I'm scared shitless, almost paralyzed in place and can't even gather myself enough to come up with a plan. Plus I don't know where to go. In training, the only advice the guards gave us in case of this situation was to lock yourself in an empty cell and hope and pray that the inmates don't overthrow the computer command center or get the keys.

"Come on."

"W-w-where?" I hate how he brings out my stutter. It's only a nervous stutter, because looking at him is like coming face to face with the devil. Perfect temptation, perfect sin. You know he is bad, but you can't help but try to take a bite. He is holding out his hand for me and taking it feels like I just sealed the deal for my soul. The alarms are blaring and inmates are shouting, but all I can hear is him, all I can see is him. But do I trust him? I guess now I have no choice.

"We need to get outta this fucking room, and outta this fucking place." He barks out like it isn't obvious that we need to get outta here.

"We can run."

"Your legs are too short to keep up with me, if I carry you like a kid with your legs wrapped around my waist then you can watch my back. Only solution because if I throw your ass over my shoulder, my center will be thrown off and we need to be fast."

I burst out laughing. I mean seriously, I know I am short, hell I have been called it all my life but seriously carry me like a kid? Clearly we need to think of a better plan. I think the stress of the situation is getting to me because I can't stop laughing. Before I can stop he has swooped down, picked me up like a mother does with her kid, one handed with me sitting on his hip and we are out the door and running for the emergency exit.

"Where the fuck to, Olivia?" He doesn't even sound breathless with the extra hundred and some odd pounds on his hip. I tell him to turn left and head towards the clinic. Seems as if some of the inmates have started a riot. Guards and inmates are fighting, inmates are completely destroying the cells. It's pure and total chaos, a level of anarchy I have never seen before.

Getting to the clinic door Damian is still carrying me as if I weigh nothing and we burst through expecting to see fighting or something. As soon as I come to the med room door I see the key sitting in the lock, and I hope and pray that Cori and Mary are safe. If anything happens to Cori, it will be pure devastation to me, it would be like losing a sister.

"Damian, put me down!"

"I like carrying you, then I know you're safe. That's all that matters is that you are safe."

"Stop, you can't say that, put me down!" I can't believe it, but I can feel a flood starting in my panties. I feel dirty about that, a man just died in front of me, and here I am getting turned on by a man who barely speaks. But the mixture of adrenaline and lust is a heady combination within me. My mind is swollen with sex on the brain.

Reluctantly, he puts me down. I turn the key and we step into the med room, quickly locking the door behind us. Fortunately, there is a side room that has no windows, so people can't see us if we are in that room. I scan the clinic looking for Cori or Mary, but I don't see them. So far the inmates haven't broken in the med clinic, but it's just a matter of time before it happens, because a lot of them are drug addicts. I try to call out for help but the phone is dead. The inmates must have found the internal grid system, which is scary because that means they can control doors, phones, and outer gates. So now, we are at their mercy. Well, him, I guess. I can only imagine that we are the puppets and Xavier is pulling our strings.

"Fuck, fuck!" I yell into the room as if the room is responsible for this mess.

"Shhhh, keep your fucking voice down. We don't need anybody looking for you in here. You shouting out fuck is going to bring people here. What's wrong anyways?" he says, almost sounding annoyed.

"Phones are down, which means the inmates have gotten inside the grid system, so they can control who comes in or out. I just hope the cops were contacted before they got into the grid." He just nods at me but doesn't seem fazed by all this. My insides are screaming at me that this guy, even though the hottest I have seen in a long time, is still an inmate. My heart is saying trust him, but my brain is telling me I'm stupid. He could be in on this and just trying to get me alone to do whatever. Not happening, buddy. I check my pocket and make sure the Dick Punch is right where I might need it. I know that I could not fight my way past all of these guys to get my ass out of here, but I will die trying. Jack is way too precious to live without a mom or dad.

Sweat is pouring into my eyes and I realize I still have my gear on. Taking off my spit shield then my flak jacket I hear a groan, almost like a growl. Looking up I lock eyes with Damian, his eyes look hungry, like at any second he could pounce and fuck me senseless. I wouldn't mind that, but now is not the time nor the place for it. I can feel my nipples harden, and I am not sure if it's because of him or if it's because I am hot and sweaty and taking off the jacket cools them, but they are two hard points begging for attention. I'd like to think it's the latter. Damian is still looking at me like a lion spotting a gazelle.

I start looking around for more weapons without letting Damian in on what I'm doing. Just because he got me out of there by doing a toddler carry doesn't mean I'm gonna put my life in his hands. Besides, he could be working with Xavier. While I'm searching, I am trying to think back on the few self-defense classes I took at Newt's Dojo. Wish I would have stuck with it, but oh well now, can't go back with the should haves, could haves, or would haves.

Going to the needles case, I find the largest bore needle I can find and I unwrap them, but not uncapping them and put them in my pockets. Then I start thinking of what kind of drugs I can use to hurt someone. Hitting up the morphine I start putting bottles in my pocket with the needles. Damian is looking at me as if I have lost my mind, but I am not going to be caught off guard. A good shot of morphine to the heart and that person can meet a certain death.

DAMIAN

What the hell is this bitch doing? We are trapped in a small room off of the room with the medicines and she is acting like an asylum patient. Dunno what the fuck is wrong with her, right now, don't care. I just need to make sure we stay safe, make sure that we get the hell on out of here. But my mind is a jumbled mess of trying to figure out a way out of this mess and trying to restrain myself from fucking her. Even though I know she would be a good lay, now isn't the time, contrary to what my dick thinks. My dick keeps stirring in her direction like it knows something I don't.

She looks like she is starting to panic, moving around the room at lightning speed. Can't say that I blame her, but sadly enough, I have been through this situation before. She's starting to pull things out like needles and bottles of medication. I think she is thinking that's going to help her. I will let her do what she needs to keep herself calm, but let's face it, a bottle of drugs is not going to stop an attack. Man, her ass looks incredible in those scrub pants. I haven't been able to look at her ass too much due to hours of not seeing her and when I do, she's always wearing that flak jacket that looks like it weighs her down. Seeing her ass now without the jacket in the way, my dick is hard to the point of pain. I feel like at any second the seams are going to rip on this uniform and my cock will be pointing in her direction, like an arrow.

Oh shit, she's looking at me like she is expecting an answer to an unheard question. I didn't even know she was talking to me, I was so lost in my head thinking about her perfect ass. Now I gotta find some way to play this shit off, and I need to re-adjust my dick in my pants. "What did you say?"

"I said what are we going to do now? I don't have the answers, and you certainly weren't going to find them on the backside of my pants." Busted. Oh well, she has to know that her ass is amazing. The perfect size and shape to admire while she is on all fours.

"It's a nice ass, and it's been awhile since I have seen one so nice." Her cheeks start to pink up, but her eyes are radiating anger.

"I bet it has, why are you in prison anyway?" Ouch, that hurts. She looks at me like I am an inmate, and she kind of has a curling to her lips like she is disgusted. But when I look into her eyes, man, it has a heat to it that I can't explain. Like at any second she is going to jump on my dick. Wishful thinking on my part, but I would seriously knock the stick outta this bitch's ass. It would be my pleasure to make her scream my name over and over again. But she is not that kind of girl, the kind you have a one night stand with. She's the kind that wants the kids, picket fence, and a dog. I have to remind myself to not put the moves on her because that is not my idea of a future. If she wants a little fun, though, I could be down for that.

"Doesn't matter, wouldn't change your views of me anyways."

She softens her face a little bit, "I don't know about that, you did save my life back there. Even though monsters exist in this place, I haven't yet been given a reason to believe that you are one."

"Don't worry about it, we need to come up with a plan."

Cocking her head to the side she says, "What kind of plan?"

"The kind that doesn't get us killed, sweet cheeks. The kind that lets us both walk out alive. That kind of plan."

She gives me an evil eye, sort of the same look my mom used to get when she wanted me to cut something out. Didn't work then, her look won't work now. But damn if it doesn't make her look hot. It seems as if my brain is being driven by my cock right now. Like it knows there is a woman in the room and its acting like a heat seeking missile going straight for her heart.

"Is there an emergency exit map in this room?" When she stares at me with a blank expression, I feel myself sighing. "You know the kind that tells you which way to go if there is an emergency like a fire? Supposed to be posted on the wall."

"Oh, I forgot about that, it's over here" she points to it. Going to look at it, I ask her where the grid system is, and once she shows me a sense of dread fills me. It's near the only emergency exit out of the prison unless we cut the gate, and then you still have the barbed wire fence to deal with. There is no way I can get us past Xavier and the inmates to get us safely out. So now I need to think of a plan B.

Olivia

Watching him as he paces about the room and all I want to do is see what's underneath the prison clothes. I bet it's good, well hell I have seen him down to his boxers, but I want to see it all. He seems like the kind of man who can move what he has and can make a woman scream. Maybe it's the adrenaline, maybe it's just my cobwebbed vagina, but all I can think about is jumping him. Well, that's not entirely true, I keep thinking about Jack, but that makes me want to cry so I would much rather think about getting some. Even if I truly wanted to, I can't because for one he's an inmate, for two, the prison has strict rules about it and I can't lose this job. Not that it matters in the heat of this moment, we are in a precarious situation.

"Olivia! Olivia! Where the hell are you?" Josh is screaming, looking for me.

"Right here, Josh." He has the good sense to look relieved, but I feel in my gut that he is anything but. Once he sees Damian in the room with me, his whole demeanor changes. He becomes rigid and stands up straight like it would make him appear bigger than he is. Hard to do with Damian being as tall as he is, and he has a stronger build than Josh. If Damian is a tree, tall, strong and solid, then Josh is a sappling.

"What the hell is HE doing here?" he says, looking at Damian as if he was nothing more than a common street dog. The way he says 'he' is dripping with disdain and full of derision.

"HE helped me when this shit all started!" I point to Damian, who is just standing there looking all bunched up. His shoulders are tight, his fists are clenched, and his nostrils are flaring. He looks like an angry bull ready to charge.

"Olivia, you need to step away from him right now!" Josh is trying to assert authority, like that would work on me. He's not my husband, boyfriend, brother or dad.

"No, Josh, you don't understand. He helped me, he got me out, and he brought me here. If he hadn't that psycho, Xavier would have killed me for sure by now. It's bad enough he already killed Burton. He was on fire, Josh, the smell, oh god the smell! It was the worst thing I have ever seen. He screamed and writhed around. He is dead because of me, his flesh came off on my hand because of me! This whole fucking mess of a situation is because of me!" I'm starting to get hysterical and panicking. I feel like the walls are caving in, and I can't catch my breath.

"Sweetheart, you need to calm down, look at me." Damian is trying to talk me down the ledge that I seem to be metaphorically standing on. When I don't look at him, he roars, "Look. At. Me. Do it now Olivia, look at me, only me." I swallow huge gulps of air, hoping to expand my lungs enough to fully breathe. Damian is standing in front of me gently stroking my arm. "Shh, shh, shhh it's ok, you're safe. I got you, I won't let anyone get to you." I don't know why he is comforting me. A man died because of me. Yes, Xavier killed him, but essentially I lit the match by provoking Xavier every time I saw him. I don't know if Burton had a family, but if they did, it's too much to bear.

"Olivia, sweetie, calm down, you have got to calm down. This isn't going to make things easier." Josh says, which is completely the opposite of soothing. It makes my skin crawl thinking about him trying to comfort me. He is fulsome and arrogant.

"What do you want, Josh?" Damian asks coolly, still stroking my arm. Just his fingertips on me has my mind racing. I'm caught in a freefall thinking about Burton, his death, and Damian. Burton wasn't always the greatest guard, but he certainly didn't deserve to go out that way. Nobody does.

"You don't get to fucking talk to me, convict. Now open the door and let me in."

Damian just rumbles at him, deep from his chest, like he cannot deal with Josh right now and a growl wouldn't cut it. I feel like I am calming down, so I step away from Damian and start walking to the door to let him in.

"No, Olivia, don't let him in." Damian says but makes no move to explain why. I'm not understanding.

"Why not, Damian?"

"Because I think he's working with Xavier."

"No, Josh wouldn't do that, he's a prick but he wouldn't do that." I'm looking at Josh as I say it, but even

I don't believe my words, they taste like poison coming off my tongue. Josh rolls his eyes at my words but says nothing to dispute it.

"Olivia, why would I work with them? What reason have I given you that would make you think that I was? I'm a prick like you said, but I'm not the criminal here, he is. Think about it, Olivia, he was cell mates with the guy for Christ's sake. If you could trust anyone, shouldn't it be with a colleague and not some inmate?" he says with a sneer. I've never noticed how ugly his face gets when he is talking about an inmate. I know he doesn't like Damian, but he did nothing to him, so why all the hate?

"What is it you want, Josh?" Damian snaps out.

"Open the door and let me in."

As I go to open the door, Damian stops me. "If this fucker tries anything, I won't hesitate to hurt him and put him out of his miserable fucking life."

I don't know what to say to that. I unlock the door but make sure that I secure the keys in a woman's best hiding spot, between my tits. Neither of the guys notices, or if they did they didn't gawk at me doing it. Damian and

Josh are staring each other down. I half expect them to whip their dicks out and see whose is bigger.

"Guys, seriously? I'm sure you both have big dicks and hangy balls, so stop with the pissing contest, and let's start planning on how we are going to get the fuck out of here."

Damian smiles, briefly, just a flash of teeth and then it's gone. Josh apparently is offended. "Olivia, your mouth, is seriously un-ladylike."

Oh well, during these circumstances he can kiss my ass. I want out of here, I want to hold Jack and never let him go. Just thinking about him makes me tear up. I want, no I need to see my baby again. And I will damn make sure I get my ass out of here alive. I also need to find Cori and Mary. Even if I have to kill everyone myself.

"Olivia, there is no plan," Josh says to me, sounding annoyed that I would want a way out of here.

"I want a plan, a plan that gets me out of here and back to Jack." I start to get angry. I notice Damian is looking at me in an odd way. I only realize then, that he had no idea about Jack. I can see he's getting mad, why I have no idea, he's not my man and he's not paying my bills. But I humor him anyways. "Jack is my son." The look on his face is comical, but given our situation I find no humor in it.

"Olivia, you should not be sharing personals with inmates," Josh chastises me as if I am a child.

Ignoring him, because he adds nothing to my thought process, I go about thinking of what the hell we are going to do. Phones are down, who knows if the inmates are even still here they could have run out the gate for all I know. Deep down, I know that's not the case, though. They are still here, well at least Xavier is still here.

"We need to get closer to the control room, that way we can trigger the gate and get ourselves out. Come on Olivia, let's go." Josh grabs my arm and starts pulling me toward the door. I jerk my arm to get away because his grip hurts, and I don't want to go with him. His plan sucks, and why would I run towards the danger. We know that they have overthrown the center, why would I want to go to them?

"Let her fucking go before I rip your arms off and beat you with them," snarls Damian.

He looks deadly serious, his beautiful blue eyes are blazing, almost like glowing ice. It's so eerily beautiful and dangerous. He looks deadly like a cobra ready to strike. I shrink when I hear him speaking, almost like a wounded dog. Even though his words aren't for me, they still have an effect on me. I shiver out of fear or being turned on. I can't quite decide which.

"The fuck are you going to do about it, convict?"

I yank my arm away and stand in between them. This doesn't need to be a pissing match. The three of us are all needing to be in this together, and fighting each other will solve nothing.

"Come on, Olivia, let's go and get the hell out of here," Josh is still imploring me to go. "Olivia you can't possibly want to stay here with him, I know somewhere we can go. We can get out of here." Josh seems to be trying to reason with me. Something is off, and I narrow my eyes at him.

"Why didn't you say that earlier? Why can't the three of us go? What are you playing at Josh?"

"Nothing. Never mind, don't fucking worry about it. Let them come get you sitting in here rotting away, no skin off my fucking teeth." Never have I ever seen that nastiness from Josh. Yes, he is a prick, but he has never been spiteful and downright ugly.

"Fuck off, Josh. I guess your true colors are shining through. You are a prick, always were a prick, and I am so glad that we only had one date." Just as my jabs are beginning to flow like a river toward this bastard, I hear a staticky crackling over the loud speaker.

"Come here cunt. Here pussy, come here." I recognize that voice, it's Xavier. I'll take one guess as to who he is talking about. I look over at Damian and his jaw is clenched, and looking back at Josh, he has a smirk on his face.

"Well, now I know why you don't want to leave this room," the prick says almost chuckling. "That's my cue to go, Olivia, please come with me, this is your last chance." For a second he sounds genuine, but I'm sure that it won't last. He is a slimy snake, and I am so glad I never gave him the cookie. If I would have slept with this guy, I am so sure it would have been terrible.

"I'm sorry, Josh, but I'm not leaving without Damian and a plan!" I stress the last word in the hopes that he will understand that we need a plan to get through this.

"Your loss."

He has me open the door and lock it again. Turning toward me I notice the sinister look in his eyes and as he fishes in his pocket, pulling out a cell phone. Odd, we aren't allowed to carry cell phones in the prison, it's against the rules. He turns his back to us as he dials a call.

"Yeah, X I found her. She's in the clinic locked in the med room. She's still got your cell mate with her. Yeah, when you get him, I want a fucking crack at him." Then he turns around and does a little three finger wave and walks to the door leading to the yard. How dare he! I'm sure my jaw has hit the floor. I didn't see that coming! Now we are just sitting ducks waiting for Xavier to get his ass in here. I can't help but yell back at him before he gets outside.

"What the fuck did you just do, Josh?"

"Xavier came to me about this a little bit ago. Asked me if I would help him. At first I wouldn't do it because I actually liked you, Olivia. But now that I see you are hung up on a fucking inmate, I knew I could accept his money. I gave you a chance to come with me, I was going to say screw him and we could have grabbed Jack and ran. But no, you are hung up on some fucker that probably murders and rapes women!" His face is red and angry as he makes his admission. Then he walks out the door.

That motherfucker! How could he? Now, Xavier knows where we are, not that it would have been hard to find if he has the camera feeds up. There are certain dead spots throughout the prison, but the med room is not one of them because of the danger that could be associated with it.

"We gotta find a different place to hide, and I would like to look for Cori and Mary. I need to know they are safe too. At least I hope they are. I would never forgive myself if something happens to them when this is all my fault."

DAMIAN

Leave it to her to think of others in this kind of situation. She blames herself for this when it's that sick fuck Xavier's fault. I need to talk to her, but first I need to get us some place safe. Since prick Josh told our location, we are definitely not safe anymore. If I ever find that pecker head, I'm going to kill him with my bare hands. I can't believe he would sell her out like that, but I guess jealousy is a strong emotion. But she stood her ground, she wasn't going to let me fend for myself in this madhouse. Honorable, yes but totally stupid. She should have ran on out of here and back to her kid. Kid, I can't believe she has a freaking kid. She must have had him real young or he's a young kid. That was a huge boner killer because I don't fuck bitches with kids, further solidifying she is not the hit it and quit it type.

"We need to make sure that we are safe before we think of anybody else. Plus I need to talk to you about something." Hoping she doesn't hear the uncertainty that is dripping from my words. Will she hate me after this is over? Can she forgive me? God only knows, I hope so.

"What do you mean we need to talk? Why not just say whatever it is you need to say, Damian, and we WILL be looking for Cori and Mary, I will not leave them here." She levels me with her stare, one that could cut you to the core. She looks pissed that I told her we needed to talk. It's not like she is my girlfriend, or that she should trust me at all, but I can't help but be worried about her feelings.

Concern is etched among her features as she is waiting for a response from me. My mouth opens and closes like a fish out of water. A burning is starting to take root in my stomach and crawls all the way up my chest. I can't believe that in all my years, I am fucking scared of this little woman. I have done far worse things in my life, and hell it's not like I have ever lied to her. She doesn't even know me, doesn't know the secrets behind these eyes. She doesn't know or understand the blood that has spilled on these hands. Yeah, we have some crazy connection, but shit, I just want to fuck her. Fuck them and leave them, hit it and quit it. I don't do relationshits, oops ships.

"We will talk once we are safe." That's all I can give her right now. Because if I start now, every secret that is within me will come spewing out at her feet.

Looking around the room, I notice that there is still flak jackets and spit shields hung on the far wall in the room on these wooden pegs. Makes me wonder if they have extras or if one of the other nurse ladies are without any kind of protection.

"Why is there so much gear here? Is that why you are so concerned about them other bitches?" As soon as the word bitches is out of my mouth, a fire lights behind her eyes. I have pissed her off. Good, because she needs to take me seriously.

"We have one extra, I just took my flak jacket off, Cori and Mary should have had theirs if they are out of the med center, but given the time this all started, Cori should have been in the yard. She should have had it on. Mary should have had hers on, but looking at the schedule she might have already left to go home. Please God." She doesn't finish her prayer only sending up a whispered plea that they are alright. She sighs in relief that at least one of them is possibly safe.

"Do you trust this Cori? Do you think she could have sold you out to Xavier?" I know she doesn't want to believe it, but after pecker head turning on us, I have no choice but to ask.

"Hell no! Cori is one of my best friends, we do practically everything together. She wouldn't sell me out. So now she is out there without any kind of protection. We cannot leave her out wherever she is. We have to find her." I am not sure I believe her, I want to, but I can't trust anybody. Except her. Only her, because she is what he wants. Hell if anything, she doesn't know me, so she shouldn't trust me.

"We will try to find your friend, but we need to go. We can't stay here. I'm thinking, as risky as it is, that we need to go back to the block. He knows we fled from there already, so maybe he won't look for us in the same spot."

"I don't know, I don't think I can go back in there. Burton's body is still there. I don't know if I can see that again." Her eyes grow wide, full of fear and worry, and her lip quivers. I don't blame her, I'm scared too, but I, of course, won't tell her that.

"Look, I don't think he will come there. I think that we can plan better when we get there, because right now we are sitting ducks just waiting for him to come along. I know we can lock ourselves in here and he can't get in, but we can't stay in here forever. We don't know if the police have been alerted, so right now that is our only option." I level her with a look of determination because I will do anything to make sure she is safe and survives this. All she does is nod.

After securing her in a flak jacket and one for myself, we leave the room and run as fast as we can back to my cell block. As I'm running, I look around at the mass destruction, bodies of both prisoners and guards scattered on the ground. Some are obviously dead, pools of blood staining the floor beneath them while others lay helplessly against the floor obviously wounded and possibly dead. But there is no time to stop running to check on their conditions.

Olivia

Running into the cell block I worry at first that the emergency exit we left through is closed again, but surprisingly it's not. As soon as we get in the door, the first thing I see is the charred body of Burton in the hallway. I wouldn't be able to recognize that it is him if I didn't see him go up in flames for myself. The smell instantly brings me to tears, it is a pungent smell. Like burning plastic and hot iron. I've never smelled anything like it. I immediately lean over and vomit all over the floor. Once the contents of my stomach have emptied, I start to dry heave.

"You good?" he asks, at least he has the good sense to not make fun of me about it.

"Never smelled anything this bad." Wiping my mouth, I need something to try to take the taste out of my mouth.

I'm watching him now, to see what the next step is. Walking through the corridor he searches from cell to cell then the guard post. Then he walks into his former cell and grabs a sheet off the bed and covers Burton. I couldn't be any more grateful at this moment, I want to kiss him. Finally, I feel like I can breathe now that Burton is covered. The smell is still in the air which I am sure will be for a very long time.

"Where can I find a bottle of water?" I ask him because let's face it, he's been living here for about a month so he should know. I need to rinse my mouth out, it tastes like someone pooped in it.

"I don't know, we weren't allowed the luxury of bottled water, but I have my cup that you can use." Walking back into his cell I can hear the sink turn on and he comes back out with a small white plastic cup. I forget that he is an inmate in all of this, but I need to try to remember that. He can hurt me in a heartbeat, but I am still not getting that vibe from him. If anything, he has shown me nothing but safety. His language is crass and he refers to women as "bitches", but I don't think he means it in a bad way.

"Now that we are a little safer, we need to come up with a plan on finding your friend and getting the hell outta here. Plus I still need to talk to you." I instantly think about finding a bed and screwing his brains out in this instance and hope that is what he wants to talk about. The tone and bass in his voice just seriously turns me on. His words feel like a soothing balm to my soul, and it goes straight to my vagina causing tingles. Funny how words that are not meant to soothe, can do just that by the timbre of someone's voice.

"So what now?" I am hoping we come up with the plan first because I feel like I am not going to like what he has to say. I feel like it is going to ruin my attraction to him, and I certainly don't want to go from liking him to hating him with just words. Or hell fearing him from what he has to say.

"Well, you said you think your friend would be in the yard, right? I am assuming since the yard is open to all the low levels that there is a room for her to be in to give out medicines. I mean she doesn't just walk up to the inmate and hand them some pills does she?" I forget that he is top level criminal and not someone who is about to get out.

Those are the guys in the yard, the ones about to leave or are non-violent.

"No of course not. There is a room that we lock ourselves into that has just a little pass window at the bottom. She is probably locked in there, but we need to get her out! It's too dangerous for her to be left out there unless there is a guard with her. But the guards don't have to stay with us, we just radio to them when we are done. What if we do Morse code on the radio? She probably won't know what it means, but it might give her hope that someone is coming!" Excitement fills my body, and I feel hopeful for finding Cori for the first time. She's my person, so she has to be ok. If she's not ok, I won't be ok, and I know Jack won't be ok. Jack still calls her his Aunt Corny, because when he was younger Cori came out as corny.

"No."

"Um, what do you mean no? Well, why the hell not?"

"Because for one, do you know Morse code?" I sheepishly shake my head no. "Didn't think so. A bunch of beeps and sounds is not going to give anyone hope. For two, hopefully she is smart enough to have her radio off and not draw attention to the room she is in. We don't want to put her in danger because we want to send a message that she probably won't hear, let alone be able to interpret."

I want to punch him in his smart mouth, then kick him in the balls. I don't see his ass coming up with any great ideas on how to find her, so until he has something, I'm just going to ignore him. He's an ass. Hot ass, but still an ass. I sit my ass on the floor of the cell block and inwardly cringe because I know that urine, feces, and splooge have made it on this floor, and inmates nor guards are notorious for their cleaning skills. Ugh, plus this flak jacket is so flipping hot. So now, I sit and wait for Captain Grumpy McDreamy Pants to come up with a plan.

Sitting here, with sweat rolling down my butt crack, I feel like it has been an eternity since the prison break began. I'm praying the cops have been alerted and have a plan in place to get the prison back under control. I start to think of Jack. He and Mom have to be going insane with worry by now. I wonder what he is feeling besides being scared. Knowing him, he will try to put on a brave face for Mom, who has to be a wreck. She seriously did not want me taking this job because of this danger right here. I have to find a way to get word to them that I am okay, that I will be coming home. I will be coming home, I just have to keep repeating that mantra to myself.

Damian has been pacing the floor looking lost in thought, hopefully thinking of a way out of this shit hole. As I sit here waiting for something to happen, like a sitting duck, I can't help but think of all the other employees here. I wonder about the warden, Rhonda. I wonder if she was even here today, and if she is, I hope she's safe. Thinking of Cori and hoping that Mary made it out brings tears to my eyes, and I try to blink them back, but it's no use. Once one tear falls, it becomes a torrent of emotion. I cry not only for myself but for Jack, my mom and the rest of the employees here. Granted I don't know who is good and who is bad, but I don't wish harm on anyone.

"Olivia, Olivia, I know you are still here." That crackling static from the intercom disturbs the calm air and my back goes rigid as steel hearing his vile voice. "Olivia, Olivia, I can't wait to do all the things I've dreamed about since I got to this shit hole. You're going to beg me to fuck you and then kill you when I finally get my hands on you. I can't wait to see the look on your face when I start to cut you to pieces. Oh, and just the thought of your eyes filled with fear as your blood drains from your body has my dick rock hard. You have me so fucking worked up, I'm almost as excited to fuck you as I am to kill you. Fuck, I might just fuck your lifeless corpse. I can only imagine how hard I'll be seeing your lifeless body in my arms. Fuck me...you have me all amped up, bitch. And when you see your blood leaking to the floor. Are you going to cry? Scream and yell? Beg me, I want you to beg me bitch."

I look over to Damian to see that his jaw is clenched and his face is red. He looks like at any second the top of his head is going to come off to release some pressure. He stopped pacing to listen to that sick fuck Xavier.

"I'm going to kill him with my bare fucking hands. He is the devil, and I can't wait to send him straight back to Hell where he belongs. Mark my words, I will have his blood on my hands before it's all over."

His words scare me and serve a sobering reminder that the guy that is quite honestly the hottest thing I have ever seen, is still an inmate. He is still dangerous. He could hurt me in an instant, but at the same time hearing his words makes me feel safer. Someone with that kind of visceral reaction cannot be all bad, granted I know he apparently did something bad to be sentenced to prison.

DAMIAN

I'm going to flay his ass open and bleed him like a deer. He will not put a hand on Olivia as long as I am around. That sick fuck has been thinking about her for almost a month, ranting on and on about her at times. I don't know why he has this obsession with her, but I can't let anything happen. I am still trying to work out a plan to get her and to get her friend out of here safely. Olivia has a son, and he needs his mother. I will not let him grow up without her.

I look over at her and she's freaking out, rocking back and forth and shaking and muttering to herself 'I will be coming home.' Tears have stained her cheeks, and she looks very pale. She is understandably cracking under the pressure, and I'm clueless how to comfort her. I don't comfort women, if she needs me to fuck the scared out of her, then I am all for it. Even an absolute wreck crying, and I'm sure there is snot involved, but even with all of that, she is still gorgeous. But I don't know how to handle this crying mess. Last time she freaked I called her a bitch. She didn't seem to like that move, so I'm just going to sit here in silence, giving her space and time.

Sitting down next to her, I slide my arm around her. Even if I don't know what to say, I am willing to be her shoulder cry on. If she needs someone to be her rock, then I will be her rock, hell I will be even better, I will be her fucking boulder. If she wants to fuck, I could do that too. Seems as if her tears have slowed since I put my arm around her. Hopefully, she is finding strength through me. The only way she will make this out relatively unscathed is to find strength.

I have something I need to tell her, but I don't think that her state of mind can handle it. I don't want her to be pissed at me that I haven't told her yet, so I am keeping my mouth shut. Sure she is going to probably hate me forever once she finds out, but she needs to know the truth.

Her head is lying on my shoulder, and all I keep thinking about is the way her tits are squished like that in her top. Which sends me into thinking what color her nipples are. I really need to stop thinking about her in that way. She sees me as an inmate that saved her. Nothing more, nothing less. I cough to try to clear the thoughts from my head before I start sporting wood at this most inopportune time. Trying to focus my mind on anything but her, I try to formulate a plan. I really need to decide on how I am going to get to Xavier. Just that thought instantly kills any desire I might have had.

I think I might have a plan on how to get to Xavier, but I can guarantee she won't like it. It might be our only shot, so she is going to have no choice but to deal. Looking out the little cell window, I notice that it is getting dark out, and the lights are not coming on. Which is not good because this shouldn't go on into the night. Night time is more dangerous because these guys have the run of the place and can pick us off from the guard tower if we go outside without the security lights on. We wouldn't even see the shot coming.

Her crying has pretty much stopped, so now I feel like maybe we can talk, gauge how she feels about the plan I have.

"So, um, can we talk now?"

"Damian, I really don't know. I don't think there is much you can say in this situation that will make me feel better."

"I'm not trying to make you feel better, but I do have some things to tell you. Some are not going to make you happy, but that's not why I am here. I am here to get you home safe and sound and that motherfucker Xavier sent to Hell."

"Why, what's in this for you?"

"Well, that's part of why I need to talk to you. I have a plan, you probably won't like it, but I don't really care." I'm being callous, I know, I just can't help it. When I look at her, it's like looking at the sun and all that is good in the world. I don't want to tarnish that or sully it with my darkness.

I glance at her before I start. "We need to find some place for you to hide, and then I am going after Xavier." Fire flashes in her eyes.

"EXCUSE ME?" she shouts back at me. I can't take the chance of someone hearing so I ask her to stop yelling. That only enrages her more.

"Fuck you, Damian, yeah put me in some hole in a box so you can go get killed by that psycho. Then what? Huh? How you gonna be a hero and save the day then when you're dead? Fuck you, I will figure a way out myself."

Her screaming only grows louder as her face goes from pale white to red hot. I know if she keeps this shit up, she'll expose us soon enough. So I do what any sane man does, I kiss the fight out of her. Her lips are soft, like touching cotton. Her mouth is clamped shut, but all I do is lick the seams and when she gasps, I strike. I thrust my tongue in and kiss her like she ought to be kissed. I can't say that the only reason I kiss her is to shut her up. I am an idiot who likes to cause myself pain.

Olivia

I have never been this thoroughly kissed before, and if his kiss is this fantastic, I can only imagine how he is in bed. Speaking of sex, I can feel his erection pressing up against me. The man definitely puts my BOB to shame. Then it occurs to me after I have tangled my fingers in his hair and am latched on like a spider monkey…that shithead! Kissing me to shut me up, although this is a kiss to end all kisses, I just want to knee him in the balls. I break the kiss by clamping down on his tongue and on first instinct I slap him. I mean seriously, yes he is hot, but he's a hot prick.

"What the fuck did you bite me for, you crazy bitch?" his voice come out as a lisp. I guess his tongue stings. Good! I hope I drew blood. A sick feeling of satisfaction slithers its way up my spine that I caused him pain. I am not a mean person, half the time I don't have a mean bone in my body. But something feels good about biting him. A little pent up aggression let its way out.

"Because! Why in the hell did you think it was okay to kiss me? Not even just kiss me, but to kiss me to shut me up! That's a dickhead move, Damian." It was an amazing kiss, best kiss I have ever had, and I want more. But he's still an inmate, even if he is my savior. My vagina is mad at me right now, I'm sure. Silence falls between us, I guess we are both lost in our thoughts. We are still sitting in this cell, and it appears to be dark outside. Hard to tell through the little window that is something like 4 inches wide and a foot and a half long, at least from this angle. I'm wondering where the cops are, I haven't heard any sirens in all of this.

"You were yelling, and I asked to get you to stop, but you wouldn't. I don't want to alert X to where we are, so I figured I would kiss you to shut you up. Better than me calling you a bitch, but you did bite me, so there is that." He's acting sullen as if my bite really hurt his feelings. Wait a minute, he called him X. I know, obviously, that X is just shortening Xavier but the way he said it sounded more like a nickname.

"Why did you call him X?"

"I dunno, didn't feel like saying Xavier, and I have heard his boys calling him X." I don't like his answer, it sets warning bells off in my gut. He's hiding something from me, and I really need to know before we go on with a plan. He walks out of the cell and starts going down the corridor.

"Where are you going?" My little legs are running to catch up to him. This is the time when I wish I wasn't so short. Such is the life and the hand God dealt me. He made me short but with good boobs, so that's a plus.

"I'm trying to find a place for you to hide at."

"I'm not hiding anywhere. He wants me, I doubt he is going to stop until he finds me. I don't want to find a place to hide when I can fight back. I'm not some weak little girl, contrary to what you may believe."

"I don't believe that you are a weak little girl, hell your bite proves you aren't weak. I just want to make sure that you get home to that boy in one piece. He needs both of his parents."

"He only has me and my mom. His dad ran off a long time ago, his loss not ours. But that is beside the point. I am not going into hiding. This prison is huge, and I am sure that I can run around all damn night and not run into Xavier." Sounds stupid even to me. I have no clue for a plan, so maybe this is the best plan possible at the moment. I still don't like it, I don't want to be shoved in some corner or closet.

"Livvy, we don't really have a choice. You are definitely not going with me to find him, and if you sit out in the open you could die. I would much rather find a spot for you to hide until I can come back and get you. I will come back for you!"

"Do not call me Livvy that is not my name!" Without even thinking my small hands connect with his thick chest as I try to shove him backward in an attempt to prove my point. TRY being the operative word. Hot damn, his chest is like a brick house! He braces his hands on his hips and glares down at me with a blank expression on his face. Immediately, I cower, realizing I've managed to piss off the only inmate in this fucking prison who doesn't want me dead. "Ok, I guess if that is the only thing we can…" my words are cut short as a blood-curdling scream fills the staticky loud speaker. My heart freezes in my chest, my lungs completely dry up, depleted of all oxygen. My head feels like it's about to spontaneously combust because I know that voice.

"Olivia, please just come and see what he needs to say!" Mary says. I can't believe she is still here. "Olivia, I am begging you. He says he's going to kill me! Please!" She's crying and it's hard to understand her, but there is no mistaking the terror in her voice. Goosebumps break out on my skin. Funny, I never thought about goosebumps happening out of fear, but it's a very real thing.

We have to do something, better yet, I have to do something. I can't keep letting my friends and coworkers get hurt over me. They all have families, and I cannot be the one which costs them their lives. I cannot let them all down, and that includes Damian. He doesn't deserve to have people die because I am too stupid to go face the consequences.

Now is the time that I know that Damian's plan won't work. I need to find Xavier for myself, but I know that Damian will never go for that. Even though I don't know much about him, he seems like the big, bad alpha type. The type that will throw his jacket down over a puddle so the girl doesn't get their foot wet. Not real life, I know, but he still seems to have that "Me He-Man" kind of mentality, beating his chest and all.

I'm lost in thought, but apparently he thinks I'm staring at his, oh God, his bulge! I just got caught staring at it, but I wasn't really. I feel the flames of embarrassment lick up my neck to my cheeks. "I wasn't staring at you, I was just lost in thought." Hopefully, he believes that.

"Mmmhmmm, sure you weren't. It's ok to stare, most ladies love to." Guess he doesn't believe me, but I also see that his ego has joined the party as well.

"I don't have time for your ego, or your dick no matter how big or small." I use hand gestures to get the small point across. Of course when I did his intake medical evaluation I saw him in his boxers so I know he is anything but small. I just want to take his ego down a peg or two. He looks like he's getting pissed, but I don't care. I just need to think. Talking about his dick is not what I want to be talking about at this moment. Maybe later once this is all over with I will think of not wanting to talk about his dick, and I will want to kick myself.

"Given the chance, baby, I would show you all the things I could do. I can make you moan, scream, bite, and blackout just from my tongue alone. You would beg me to push my cock in that overly tight pussy. Yeah, I know it's tight, because if you had a regular fucking you wouldn't be so uptight." Asshole. He's got me pissed, turned on, and ashamed at the same time. Who knew a person could go through a gamut of emotions so quick. He has a point about me being uptight, but I would never let him know that.

"How do you know that some man doesn't make me scream every night? That when I ride him, I make him pass out with how good this pussy is? That when I make him come he is breathless and whispers my name as if it's the last name on earth?"

I can see his Adams apple bob up and down, and I know that I have affected him. A small victory for me, but I will take it. "Now how do you suppose we go about killing Xavier so I can get home to my son?" I level him with my mom stare, the one that gets Jack moving and doing what needs to be done.

DAMIAN

Fuck if she ain't scary as shit when is mad. When I finally tell her the shit I need to tell her, I'm worried she might bite my head off. Her eyes are all puffy from crying and red from being mad. She looks like she is ready to chop my head off. I was just trying to get her mind off that one lady being with Xavier. I know she worries about her coworkers, I probably would too, if I had true coworkers that I cared about.

"I still say that we need to hide you, so I can go to Xavier myself." Still think that is the best plan for her. If she is in hiding, and I can have eyes on Xavier, he won't personally be able to get to her. Although, I'm not stupid, I know he has his henchmen out there searching for her.

"I don't like that idea, besides, how am I to be sure that you are not ultimately working for him? You think I haven't thought about that? Just because you got a hot body and pretty face, doesn't mean you aren't the enemy or working with the enemy!"

"Damn, if we weren't in this situation I would redden your ass for that. When have I ever given you any indication that I was working for Xavier? I never have, and I never will. He's the worst of the worst, the scum of the earth. If you knew the things I knew about him, you wouldn't want to run straight to him!" She doesn't need to know that I know Xavier way more than I am letting on.

"He rapes women, tortures them, hell I know for a fact that he has tortured teenage girls, and killed boys! One time, only pieces of the lady were found. Do I need to tell you more, because I most certainly can tell you more?" She looks a little green, good, maybe a healthy dose of what this piece of shit is capable of will scare her into not going to him.

"No, you don't need to go on. I just need to get Mary out of there, she doesn't deserve this because of me! You already said what he does to women, why would I let that happen to her?"

"She's not there because of you, she is there because of him. Don't forget that. He is the sick one here, you aren't. Now, we have been here for hours, are you hungry? I have some snacks from the canteen." She needs to eat to maintain her strength because I feel like this is going to get worse before it gets better.

"I'm not really hungry. I don't see how anyone can be hungry in this."

"Livvy, I wasn't really asking if you were. You need to eat to keep your strength up because you are going to be here for a while. I'm going to see what else I can round up instead of just snacks. I'll be right back." I want to check the area again because we have been sitting in this same spot for a while, and I want to make sure nobody is around. Plus I need to find a spot for her and check out the camera situation.

"I already told you, don't call me Livvy. I can't stand that! Don't do it again, or so help me God I will smack the taste out of your mouth." Wow, she's breathtaking when she is mad. I guess her anger is a huge turn on for me because I want to bend her over my cell bed and fuck her until she can't walk. Since I can't do that, I do the most normal thing around. I kiss her. Surprisingly enough, she is kissing me back even after the last disastrous time I kissed her. I thought she was going to fight me again, but she actually lets out a little moan. Her moan goes straight to my dick. He is eager to be let out of the confines of my pants. I guess I can take it as she's enjoying this. I kiss her as if this is a forever goodbye, one that is both breathtaking and heartbreaking. I don't know why but that burning is back in my chest.

Olivia

Oh my God, he is kissing me again. I can't help but moan and press myself harder against him. His lips are like a sinful treat. It's like tasting the finest wine, I could get addicted to these kisses. I let my hand tangle in his hair and my other starts to travel down his chest to feel his rock hard abs. I have never touched six pack abs in a non-clinical setting, and these are almost like eight pack abs. Holy shit, I didn't even know that was possible. I can't believe I am letting him kiss me. My vagina might box itself up and move out, but I have to put a stop to this.

Breaking the kiss, he rests his forehead on mine. "We can't do this. I don't know you, you're a prison inmate and with all the shit going on around us it's just wrong." I feel like if I keep saying it to myself, then I might actually believe it. Never mind the fact that I still have a hand in his hair and one on his chest, his very firm, muscular chest. God, this is so frustrating! If it was a different situation and he wasn't in prison, then I would jump him. I feel wrong and dirty for wanting him. Here Mary is being held by Xavier and his men, scared out of her wits and I am making out with a guy! Adrenaline is an extremely powerful thing, not to mention sexual attraction. This is the only plausible excuses I can come up with for the way I am acting.

"Livvy, what is so wrong with this? I know the situation isn't ideal, but I know you can feel the heat between us. Baby, you look at me like you want to eat me up. I definitely want to eat you up, sweetheart, amongst other things. When I am through with you, you won't remember my name, let alone your name. I want to taste your juices on my tongue, want to hear you moan my name, bury myself so deep in you that all you can feel is me for days. Feel your knees go out because the amount of ecstasy you feel will make you weak. I need to ruin you for any other man that once I am in you, you can't help to admit that you are mine. Because Olivia, by the time this is all over, you will be mine."

Well, shit. Is it possible to have a mini orgasm without actual touching? Because if it's possible, then that explains the tingling I got during his speech. I'm sure I look pretty stupid right now with my mouth hanging open, I just can't help it. His words, however dirty they may be, have done something to me. Not only do I want him, but I want all the things he described. I guess feeling desirable is something that I need. Kind of like when you cut your hair and you hope everyone notices. Well, it's been a long time since anyone has noticed my hair or me.

"Damian, look," I start, but he cuts me off, again. I hate that about him because it's rude. But hey, if this is the only bad thing about his personality that I am finding then I feel like I'm winning. Of course, the whole prison stay is something else altogether. I have no idea how to handle that mess. I mean seriously, I cannot date someone in prison. I'm embarrassed with myself because I can feel myself falling into the abyss that is Damian Shaw. I don't know how to handle it, and that worries me. I am a planner, I am normally solid in my feelings, but all I feel with him is confusion.

"Olivia, I am not asking for you to marry me, hell I am not the type you marry. But I do want to have some fun with you. Even though I know, this is not the ideal circumstances. But we need to have that conversation now. There are things about me that you need to know."

"Look, Damian, you seem to be a nice enough guy. I don't know what you did to land yourself in here, but it's against the rules for me to do anything with you. Plus I have my son to think about. Then we have the whole riot thing going on. It's just not smart." Hopefully, he understands Jack needs a dad, not an inmate, or someone bouncing in and out of prison.

After I get it off my chest, he is now wearing a scowl, but in his eyes he has a look of determination. Like the big bad wolf, better to eat me with. His eyes are screaming that he is going to use me up and spit me out, possibly devour me whole. I'm still not used to being looked at like that, and it makes me nervous. Like pit sweat and sweat mustache nervous.

"I'm going in search of food. Stay here and scream if you need me," he huffs out, and I can't help but feel hurt because his change of mood is because of me. I hate that I have hurt his feelings, but this can't continue.

I hate this, it's eerily silent since he walked away. It's kind of like when you are at home alone and you go to take a shower, you hear everything. My imagination starts to run wild, and I feel like I am being watched. I don't see how, there aren't any cameras in the individual cells, just cameras in the corridors. Sitting where I am sitting, I hope I can't be seen on the cameras, but I don't know for sure. But my skin is starting to crawl, and an overwhelming sense of fear has gripped me, goosebumps are running up and down my body.

I feel the need to run, but Damian told me not to leave. He wants me to scream if I need him, but I kind of feel like that would be stupid because I don't know that anyone is there. Plus the whole, I am woman hear me roar bullshit. So I sit, and I wait. But I can feel eyes on me, I just know it.

DAMIAN

After leaving Olivia in the cell, I creep through the corridor counting each camera I pass as I scour the area making sure that no one is lurking close by. I search through a few cells for some food and try to find a place to hide Olivia. Xavier will not stop at getting her, so I have to be the one to stop him. I need to be the one ahead of him if I am going to keep her safe. He cannot win this. I can't help but think of her words. She seems repulsed that I am an inmate, which is ok, hell anybody should be. But to think that I would be a bad influence on her kid, I just don't know what to think. I would be the first to tell the kid to stay the hell away from trouble. I think she is looking for a relationship, and I am just looking to get my dick wet. I mean yeah she's fucking hot, she seems like a great mother to her kid, and I'm sure she will make some man very happy to marry her. I am just not that man, and I can't help but feel sadness for that. What the hell is wrong with me? Where did the Damian go that wants to fuck any hot girl six ways from Sunday?

Walking into the guards break room, I see the fridge which I know will be a jackpot. Guards don't like to eat the food that is prepared by the inmates, so they bring their own. Don't blame the guards, sometimes those inmates will fuck with the food. Most get caught, it's really hard to try anything in the kitchen, but sometimes their hijinks goes unnoticed. Some guys will jizz in the food, some will put any drug they can get their hands on in it. Not saying it happens all the time, but it happens a lot more than these people around here realize. Seems as if someone is looking out for us in this shitty situation.

Grabbing sandwiches, soda, chips, and water, I head back to my cell. I have counted 16 cameras so far and haven't seen anybody. Fortunately, I did find a broom closet of sorts that I can stick her in, and if we are quick Xavier might not catch me doing that. Love to do more than just stick her in it and walk away, but she has made it clear she wants nothing to do with me in that way. Maybe once she knows the truth about this whole thing she will feel differently after she gets over being pissed.

Walking the corridors of this block makes me think of the short time I've been here. Am I a bad man? Some could say yes, others might say no, every bad thing I have ever done has been for a reason. I don't know which I am anymore. Growing up it used to be a clear cut answer, but as I have gotten older, now I'm not so sure. I have been in and out of places like this for so long now, that I don't know which way is up, hell I don't even remember the names of the prisons anymore. Then look at the way I treat women. Hit it and quit it, in and out, and hit and run have all been used to describe my love life. Or lack thereof, because when you hit it and quit it, it's still pretty lonely. I get what I need and send them on my way, until her. She is the first girl that I have met that I want to know more of before I fuck her. Maybe because she is unattainable, she has become a challenge to me. Don't get me wrong, she will be screaming my name soon enough, she just doesn't realize the electricity and the fire we have between us. I know when she enters a room without even seeing her, we just have this pull that I don't understand.

As I turn down the last corridor to be checked, I hear a blood-curdling scream. If it's possible, my blood turns to ice because I know who is screaming. I take off in a dead sprint towards the cell where I left Olivia. Two guys are stalking toward the cell and Olivia is screaming at them to stop and not come any closer. I feel like my stomach has dropped out of my ass because I am so scared. As I reach the cell door, I see that has his hands gripped firmly around her throat choking her, and the only sound to be heard from her lips is a desperate gurgle. Her face is a sickly shade of maroon and spittle has formed at the corner of her mouth. She is scratching and clawing trying to get some relief. It is the most terrifying thing I have ever seen. Hell, I have done some fucked up things in this life, things that would turn a person's stomach upside down. I've killed, and maimed and I will do it all over again to keep her safe.

An unexpected visitor, I punch the first guy in the back of the head and he tumbles to the ground like a ton of bricks. The scumbag who has my Olivia is still choking her, and doesn't even realize his buddy is laying on his on the floor. Olivia is still trying to scrap her way to relief. Her lip is bleeding and she looks terrified, her face is a sickly shade of purple.

"Bitch, I told you, Xavier wants you. If I let you go, you will come with me. It's nothing personal, whore, you just pissed off the wrong man when you kicked me.

Xavier wants to see you, he just didn't say you had to be in good condition when that happens."

Olivia looks beyond frightened now. I'm surprised that she hasn't pissed her pants, hell I wouldn't blame her. The dick must have loosened up his grip on her throat because she is slowly returning to a somewhat normal color and she isn't clawing at his arms anymore, more just holding onto his hands. He rears back to punch her in the face, he's quick, but I damn sure am quicker. I sneak up from behind and grab him in a headlock, and he immediately drops Olivia. She drops to all fours, gasping for air as tears stream down her face.

"Since when did Xavier send pussy bitches to do his dirty work?"

"Fuck you, Shaw, he will get to her, you know it and I know it. Fuck that whore, she's gonna get hers. He already has her friends, you think he ain't gonna kill them too? Shit, he has already started torturing them, it's only a matter of time before he gets bored and fucks them, then kills them. If he hasn't already."

"Where is he hiding?" I still have him in a headlock, but I'm not gonna kill him… yet.

"I wouldn't tell you for shit. He would fucking gut me."

I apply more pressure to his throat because apparently he is underestimating what I am going to do with him. "Motherfucker, what makes you think I'm not going to kill you?"

He looks a little scared, but he doesn't fully believe my promise. "Olivia, please go to a cell a few doors down and wait for me." I don't even look at her when I say it, I just stare into his eyes. His eyes go wide, and now apparently he believes me.

"Damian, what are you going to do?" her voice is hoarse. She sounds like she gargled broken glass, and I know it has to be hurting her to talk.

"Sweetheart, please just go." I glance over at her, she is still on the floor looking at me while she is rubbing her throat.

"B-b-but what if someone gets me in there?" The fear is evident in her eyes and in her stutter. I would give anything at this moment to take it all away. She is too pure to have such terror in her eyes.

"Nobody will because they would have come running had they heard us. But I am right here, I'm not leaving you again."

She stands to leave, but has to grip the wall to keep her balance. The lack of oxygen is probably making her a little disoriented. God, she is so strong. Her son is very lucky to have such a warrior for a mother. Even all bruised up and bleeding, she is still the most beautiful angel ever. As she is walking away, I begin to loosen my grip a little on the guy. I don't want to kill him, but I know I have to. I cannot risk him running back to Xavier.

"Look, tell me what all you know. I want to know where he is, how many are working for him. What he is doing. Tell me everything, and I might spare you." I won't, but I need his trust. Hopefully, he will tell me what he knows. I would hate to kill him without information first.

"I ain't telling you shit! You can't hurt me any worse than what he will do if I snitch." He spits towards me and it lands near my feet. I grab a hold of his hand and snap his pinkie and thumb, pulling them all the way back to his wrist. Ignoring his screams I ask him again to tell me what he knows.

"Oh God, ok, ok. Xavier is in the control room. He knows you are going to come looking for him. He fucking knows man, he knows everything about you. He knows why there is no record of what you have done. He knows it all! Fuck, just let me go."

"How many are working for him?" Just for good measure and maybe a little bit of self-satisfaction, I grab his index finger and twist hearing the satisfying crunch. He is holding his hand to his chest, but I can still see that his fingers are lying against him at an awkward angle.

"I-I-I don't know how many. He knows all about you. He knows you are a cop!" I hear a loud gasp from over my shoulder by the cell door, and my eyes automatically shut. Shit, I can feel the anger radiating off of her. I should have come clean sooner, but I know she doesn't know the whole story, I just hope she lets me tell her.

I hear groaning and realize his buddy is about to wake up. Forgot about him, but I'll deal with it as well. "Olivia, wait! You don't know the whole story! Wait!" But she runs away. I'm sure she won't go far, she's too scared. I have to deal with these two first. Since the first one is just stirring, I decide to deal with half-hand. I quickly work to beat his face to a pulp. After I stomp a new asshole in him and he's knocked out, I strip the bunks and get to ripping up sheets. I know where Xavier keeps his shanks so I grab one of the shanks and pocket the rest. Slicing into the mattress is pretty easy considering a number of people who have been on them. I start ripping the coils out. Funny how inmates in this prison don't think of these things, other prisons only have foam pads as mattresses, so it was good luck this one is so old school. Getting enough coils out, I go about making some cuffs, nothing but bent coils and sheet scraps. Not sure how long these will hold, but I am betting on that dead guard still having keys and cuffs on him.

I hate leaving those two assholes, but I need to get to the guard and see if he has any cuffs on him, and I need to find Olivia. If someone has caught up with her, I don't know what I will do. I guess rip them apart limb by limb, not that I wouldn't be so nonchalant about it. Nobody messes with what's mine. Wait, what? How is she mine? I'm stuck in this shit hole, she now knows I'm a cop, so why the hell would she be mine? Shit, she keeps pushing me away already, so she isn't mine. I will do good to remember that. She's pushing me away, not the other way around.

Olivia

What in the hell? So now he's a cop? I don't know what to think, is he dirty and that's what landed him in here? I just need to find time away from all of this just to get my bearings and breathe. This is all too much, and it needs to stop, too much to process, I'm overwhelmed. I mean seriously, how can I be so into a man who is a dirty cop? What the hell is wrong with me? I am a mother, and I have to wonder to myself would I be ok with Jack bringing home a dirty cop as a girlfriend? No, I don't think I would be.

I'm rushing through the corridor so fast, just trying to get the hell away from Damian that I trip over a crack in the concrete and fall to the floor, cutting my leg open. I know in the guard hub that a first aid kit is hanging on the wall. It seems like nothing is going well today. I'm stuck in this shit hole, a madman wants to kill me or do whatever with me, my friends are being held hostage, and my poor son and Mom are probably going crazy with worry. I just need to repeat my mantra. That is the only thing that will get me through this, and home to my Jack.

Making my way into the guard's room, I can hear someone coming down the corridor so I dash inside real quick and grab the first aid kit. Seeking safety, I crawl under the countertop that covers three-quarters of the room. My scrubs are ripped open at the knee and blood is trickling down my leg and onto the floor. If Xavier and his men want me, it's only a matter of time before the find me now. I observe the wound to my knee and know I need stitches, but that is something that will have to wait. I just need to staunch the bleeding for now.

"Olivia, I know you are still in here." I can't really recognize the voice because they are speaking so low. I keep a hand over my mouth so I don't make any noises.

"Olivia, come on, let me explain!" Now I know it's Damian.

I still don't want him to find me, but I am not going to hide from him if he comes in here, so I start working on my leg. Granted this isn't a kit issued by the clinic, this surprisingly has a lot of stuff in it. Rooting around I find a suture kit and betadine swabs. No pain meds, but I do have that morphine shot, so I could probably give myself a little just to dull the pain. But I don't want to do that because I need to have my wits about me. Sounds like a great idea, though, just a little escape away from this situation. Rubbing the swabs along the sides of the wound, then in the wound to cleanse it I see him.

Nostrils flaring, eyes blazing, he looks like a man who is going insane. His eyes are a blazing blue that looks like glaciers you see on TV, or the crystal clear water you see at islands not touched by our pollution. He steals my breath with just one look, instantly making me hot all over. I duck my head to remove myself from his steely stare, and I gulp in a huge breath. I see him walk towards me and crouch down, but I still can't look him in the eyes. Every time I do, my heart hurts and I can't look away, like some trance that he has put upon my heart and body. But my body, my body is acutely aware of his presence even though my eyes aren't drinking him in.

"Who did this to you?" He seems to be choking on his words. He hooks his fingers under my chin, forcing me to look up.

"I did it to myself, now what do you want, Damian? Or should I say, Officer Shaw?" Low blow, but he deserves it, I can see the hurt in his eyes.

"Cut the shit, Livvy."

"You lied to me and you want me to cut the shit? Doesn't work that way, asshole!" I'm seething! I trusted this man and he didn't tell me. Granted, it's not a life-changing never forgive the person again secret. But it's something I should have known. Dirty cops have a hard enough time in prison, I just feel like he should have told me already. The target pinned on our backs just keeps getting bigger and bigger.

"I never lied to you. I just didn't tell you, big difference, babe." Cocky asshole. I hate him right now. He is acting like it's not bothering him, but his eyes betray the cockiness. I realize that he cares what I think of him, and butterflies stir in my stomach at that revelation.

"You omitted the truth, which makes you a huge asshole in my book. I don't date assholes or dirty cops. Ya know, Damian, I wouldn't have been so mad had you told me when all of this mess began. But you kept hiding it from me."

"Watch your mouth, Livvy. I kept telling you that we needed to talk, but every time I said it, you blew me off."

He squats down beside me and grabs my calf, I instantly feel a flood in my panties from his touch, making me forget about my calf bleeding. Taking the swabs from me he starts cleaning my cut. I hiss through my teeth because it's cold and he's rough. He just mutters a harsh "sorry" to me. Through the pain, I still don't want him to stop. I want him to lay me down and show me what a night with him could be like, how rough he really could be.

Getting that feeling of not being able to breathe again, I pull my leg away. "Hand me that suture kit, this needs stitches."

"I'll do it."

"Umm, no thanks, I would much rather do it myself, that way I know it's right."

"God dammit, Livvy! I learned how to suture, ok? So let me fucking do it." Smirking at me as he says that. I wish I could go all female praying mantis and bite his flipping head off!

Handing over the suture pack, I feel like my head is spinning with thoughts of Damian being in the forefront of my mind. I know I should be thinking of getting home to Jack, or hell even getting out of this alive. But when he touches me, all fades away except for thoughts of how we could make each other burn in pleasure. I wonder if I have lost too much blood and it's making me woozy, or if it's just him. He warns me ahead of time that this shit is going to hurt. I guess it just didn't register in my mind how much it would. I scream out because shit that hurts, my screams echoing down the corridors of the cell blocks.

"Livvy, you have to be quiet because anybody can hear you. I know it hurts, babe, just bear with me. It will all be over soon."

I whimper because that is all I can do. I want to scream and beat him and claw his eyes out, but I know I can't. Tears are streaming down my face and splattering onto my shirt.

"Here, take my shirt, it gives you something to bite down on."

Oh good lord! He rips his shirt over his head in that way all guys do, where instead of grabbing from the bottom they grab from the back, and for some odd reason

I find so hot. His tattoos are on glorious display, and I want to trace the words with my tongue. Never thought I would be envious of cartoon characters running up and down his bicep, but I am. His rock hard abs are just begging for me to rub my fingers up and down them, maybe use my nails. His shirt which is nothing but prison-issue garb smells like him, musky and like the woods. Even though he has cheap soap, it smells delicious. It is just him, and I want him now. I hear him clear his throat, but I can't stop staring at him.

"Livvy, I'm going to keep going. Just wanted to prepare you, but you don't have to stop looking at me. I know now though that I will get in that pussy before the end of the day. I will hear you whisper my name. Of course it can only be a whisper because you will have no voice by the time I'm done with you."

Oh my, I feel like a flood has opened up in my panties, hot tingles snake up and down my spine. I want him, like seriously want him. It's been so long, I worry if I could keep up with him. He has already said all he does is fuck women and leave them, can I be alright with that? I don't know the answer to that because I feel like if I do give in that he will ruin me. Not just in a professional sense, because dating an inmate let alone a crooked cop could tank my career. I feel like he could ruin me from the inside out. Like he would crush my soul if he decided I wasn't good enough. He is so all-consuming, you notice him immediately in a room and not just because of his size, but this aura he carries about him.

Never had I have any self-confidence issues, and never once have I hung onto a man just because I didn't want to be alone. I know who I am and what kind of woman I am, and I have to decide if he is good enough to be what I need. I need a strong man, one who can take care of me in the bedroom and take care of what needs to be done outside of it too. Someone who not only wants me but wants to be a father figure in Jack's life. Someone who won't run when the going gets tough. So thinking of what I want, the answer to him and I trying to make a relationship work would be no. Can I have a good time, fool around with him and then be done? I could, as long as I am in the right mind frame for it. Too many women have fallen for the booty call, we all know that girl. I cannot be the type of girl that pines after a boy who wants nothing to do with her besides what's in between her legs.

As he works on my leg, I'm so lost in thoughts and decisions that I'm numb to the pain. I barely see what he is doing, even though it looks like I am staring right at his hands. He has wonderfully strong hands, the kind that you want all over your body or plunging into your hair to pull your head back so that he can taste your lips. Hands that look like they could hurt someone, or hold someone to ease any pain. Hands that you can feel every ridge and callous of the skin because he works so hard with his hands. Sexy hands, hands that I want holding onto me.

I have no idea why I am feeling the way I am feeling. He has given me zero indication that he is looking for a relationship with me. If anything he has warned me off, he's told me that he is a hit and run kind of guy. I feel like I am over thinking things. I know he finds me attractive, I have seen the tent he has pitched in his shorts. The kisses we have shared have been something so close to electricity I am surprised we didn't cause a power outage from the surge. I guess this lust I'm feeling is something different than the lust one feels when they see a hot guy. This one is real and in my face.

I hear a little chuckle and my daydream snaps. My cheeks heat up because he has caught me staring. I can't help it, he's fucking hot. Sweat beads at the base of my spine and work its way down. What feels like gravity pulls me towards him. Towards touching his lips that are so soft, so warm, and so fulfilling.

"Baby, all done." he murmurs, I don't quite catch what he is saying because I am caught in a war between his lips and his eyes. His eyes hold every emotion he has, crystal blue and unearthly, his lips are in a slight smirk, and I want nothing more than to lick and suck on his full bottom lip.

"Livvy, I'm going to kiss you now," he says as he leans toward me expectantly. I guess he is giving me the chance to stop him.

I have no choice but to give in. He is an enigma, I can't figure him out. It's like my mind and my heart are warring with each other, and I can't for the life of me figure out why my heart is in this. I shouldn't have feelings for him. He's dangerous and wrong in the worst ways possible. But, I can't help it, he has infiltrated everything within me.

As soon as his lips touch mine, I shift my body so that I am straddling him. He is warm, and inviting, and he is everywhere. Taking over every sense I have, and apparently ruining any good sense I ever had. I have to touch those abs, I have to feel his skin. A need to rake my fingers over his chest takes over, I want to cause him a little pain. He is so warm and smooth with just a light smattering of chest hair and a happy trail that makes me want to lick all the way down. His chest hair is perfect, just enough to touch, but not enough to get my hands caught in. Scratchy, and I just want to rub my face up and down his chest like a kitten.

We are a tangle of arms and legs, trying to get close to each other, because even though I am already in his lap, it doesn't feel close enough. He reaches for my scrub top to pull it over my head, and a tiny modicum of moral thought jumps into my mind. By then, my shirt is over my head and he is licking his way down. My nipples poke through my bra like two beacons showing him the way. Of course, he doesn't seem to need any directions because just sitting here with his hands on me can make me orgasm without him even breaking into the waistband of my pants.

His hands are just lightly grazing my sides, more like a caress instead of manhandling. For some reason, this turns me on even more. I can feel his dick poking through his pants, and knowing that I turn him on too is a strangely empowering feeling. Like a lioness stalking her prey. I need to feel him, taste him, and touch his skin. Running my hands up and down his pecs and abs, I am in heaven. His tongue licks down my neck, and I can't help the moan and shivers that results. I need to feel him inside of me.

Grabbing for the waistband of his pants, my nerves take over. Breaking our kiss, our magical, wonderful, angels singing up above kiss, he looks at me. Really looks at me. I feel like he is seeing everything about me. All the struggles, loneliness, and defeat. He sees the strength, the boldness in me. He sees everything. It all makes my heart soar, my soul sing, tears forming and all of that mushy shit. Maybe because it's been so long since I have gotten laid that I have turned into some girly girl. I have to remember who I am because I feel like with him I could get lost forever. Then where would that leave me? In love with a prison inmate, not only that, a dirty cop.

"Are you sure you want this?" he questions, I guess he can see the internal struggle that I'm having. I feel like I should come clean and tell him that this will be a one-time thing. But that would surely kill the mood. He has said before that he is not the relationship type, but bringing it up right now while I am straddling him and we are both topless would just bring negativity into this beautiful situation. Our surroundings are not beautiful by any means, but being in his arms, close to each other is a breathtaking experience.

"Shut up and fuck me. Let's get the passion we feel for each other out of our system once and for all so we can go back to finding a way out of here." I moan out the last few words, as he swirls his hips and thrusts against me, hitting all the right spots.

Of course, I guess my bluntness has killed the mood some because he takes my arms and holds them at my side.

DAMIAN

What the fuck? I'm used to being the one who will hit it and quit it, never have I ever had the move pulled on me. It is an instant boner killer, and I can't quite figure out why. Seriously, what more could I ask for? A hot piece of ass is practically throwing herself at me, I haven't fucked in a month, and my dick *was* about to bust out of these pants. But then she said what she said. Does she really think I am that big of scum that I am just trying to get my dick wet? I mean, normally, yeah that's me, but not with her. She's too precious, too special, like delicate glass. On one hand, I don't want to shatter her, but that little devil on the other shoulder is telling me to just do it. Shatter her into a million pieces, get what I want and move on.

"Look, Livvy, I know you think I am some scumbag, but I promise you once you hear what I have to say you won't think I am. Well not too big of one. You just need to listen to me."

"Stop fucking calling me Livvy, it's not my name." Even angry she grinds against me. Shit, I can't take this, there is a pull in me that has to just fuck her and then we will deal with the aftermath later. I have to know what she feels like, because with her right here in my arms, I feel like the strongest man in the world. Like I could take a bullet and keep coming at you. It's an intense pull, a deep attraction that I can't deny. Something within me belongs at this moment with her.

Going in for the kiss again, I feel like I need to take my time with her, show her that I am not the bastard she thinks I am. I need to make sure that she is fully satisfied before I take what I want. Needing to caress her, I pull her hair back over her shoulders and start kissing down her face and neck. Her tits are pushed up against my chest and unclasp her bra, needing to feel the weight of them in my hands. So soft and warm, but with a heft to them that I am not used to with the women I fuck. I guess I just never paid attention to their chests before. Her nipples are a beautiful dusky rose color, and she must be wearing perfume when I pop one of her nipples into my mouth it is the sweetest taste. Like peaches with honey on them.

Palming her other breast with my hand and sucking on one, I feel like I could blow my load. Long gone are the thoughts of her boner killing comment. Long gone are the thoughts of getting us out of this situation and getting my hands around Xavier's throat. I can't think of anything but her at this moment. She moans as I give my attention to her chest, and it is like an electric zing straight to my dick. At any moment, my dick is going to bust the seams on my pants and find its way to her wet heat, like finding its home. Not wanting her other nipple to feel left out, I start in on that one and palming the other like before. Her moans are out of control, and I am worried about someone hearing us. Just my luck I will get us killed while naked. I guess not the worst way to die with my dick inside of her, but still not on my list of ways.

Holding her close to my chest with her legs wrapped tight at my waist, she pulls my hair hard as my teeth scrape down her throat. Motherfuck! I really don't embarrass myself like a 15-year-old boy and blow my load, but at the rate she's going anything is possible. As my mouth finds its way down to her tits, I pull her nipple between my lips and bite down. She instantly moans louder. I guess this girl likes it dirty. She doesn't know what she is getting herself into with me.

"Hold on," I growl because I am not about to lay her down on a dirty prison floor. I guess I am going soft in my stay here, but she deserves better. Grabbing some blankets from the excess bin that the guards have, I lay them out on the floor.

She goes to take off her pants and I immediately stop her with my giant hand on top of her tiny one. I want to be the one to take her pants off, to touch all the way down her body. "Is something wrong?" she asks with uncertainty in her voice. She doesn't get it. Her uncertainty makes me want to devour her. Her uncertainty makes me want to take everything away from her. It makes me want to be the devil and rip every bit of good from her and keep it for myself. But the devil in me has to wait, because I can't, no I won't do that to her. I guess she has a stronger hold on me than I realized.

"No, I just want to be the one to touch you. To bring you to the point of no return, Livvy. To be the one to take you so far, where all of your thoughts are me and only me." I can see that she is visibly clenching her legs together. She may say she doesn't like me calling her Livvy, but I can tell it really turns her on. Hooking my fingers into her waistband, I slowly pull her scrub pants down her legs. She is squirming under my ministrations. A side of me comes out that I never thought would happen with a woman. I want to protect this woman at all costs. I want to own this girl, be inside her forever. I know that once I get into that pussy then I will feel heaven.

As I get her pants to her creamy thighs, I almost lose my shit. I feel like a superhero, I feel like I could beat my chest and spray my seed all over her like a barbarian. I want to claim her so that nobody else could ever see her again. How could this be happening? I am not a picket fence and kids kind of guy, but looking at her as I slide my fingers down her legs to get her pants off, I feel like I could be with her.

Olivia

Why did he stop? He must have something wrong with his dick, some erectile dysfunction or needs a little blue pill. Something, because right now my need is bleeding through my pores. I am so turned on that if he doesn't get to it, my hand will find its way down my pants and I will be taking care of my own business. Figures the first time I get laid in so many years and the guy can't keep it up.

"Ummm, is something wrong?"

"I'm just trying to keep control here. I want nothing more than to rip these clothes off of you with my teeth and do things to you that will make your scream. That when we get out of here and you are old and grey you will still remember this exact moment. So yes, somethings wrong. I can't do all the things I want to do to you here in this shit hole." Shit that is hot, and probably the most words I have ever heard him say. I'm finding that when he speaks, it is something that should be listened to. He doesn't seem to waste his words with everyday conversation.

He pulls my pants down past my knees, and instantly I see his nostrils flare and his eyes widen. Knowing that I am not growing a troll down there, I know what he sees. My blue cotton panties are soaked through with my arousal. Hopefully, that will get his dick hard again.

"I can smell how much you want me, how much you need me. Don't worry, baby, the feeling is mutual. That ache you feel? That ache will go away soon, I'll make sure you get your fill."

I have no retort for that. He's absolutely right, I do want him. The scent of my arousal is hanging in the air, a sugared smell, just waiting for him to take me and give me what I need.

"Damn, you are going to be the death of me, Livvy. I have never smelled anything so sweet, so good. I can't wait to taste you, I have to know if you taste as good as you smell."

Dumbfounded by his words, but turned on still, I have to clench my thighs together. His words are like kisses on my skin and goosebumps break out. I have to have him between my thighs and quick or I will come apart.

Placing his body between my thighs he presses his nose against my panties and sniffs. My legs almost close around his head because the tiny bit of air disturbance has me trembling. It's been so long since a man has been between these thighs that I worry that I won't be good enough.

"Livvy, I need you to relax. Please, baby, just relax for me. You are fusing them thighs together."

"Oh, sorry, it's just been awhile since I have had sex with anyone, so I'm just outta practice." My cheeks heat at my admission.

"Don't worry, I'll be very gentle." he says with a Cheshire cat grin. I don't believe him for a minute.

He slowly drags my panties down my thighs leaving me naked and exposed to him when he hasn't even taken off his pants yet. He is moving painstakingly slow, letting my body burn in the moment. That's when another thought crosses my mind and has me drawing my knees to a close and I start to sit up.

"The fuck do you think you're doing?"

"We don't have a condom. So sorry, as much as I want to, no go between these legs, hot shot."

"Livvy, you and I both know that there is more ways to make you come than my cock filling you up. Why, Sweetass, do you think I haven't taken my pants off? I know, no glove, no love."

Cocky son of a bitch! I want to kick him in his baby maker, but that won't take the cockiness from him. But before I get the chance to do just that, he kisses me. In a kiss that feels like he is stealing my soul, he makes my toes curl, and has me wrapping my legs around him in an effort to get closer to him. He reaches around and grabs my hair closer to my scalp and gently pulls. I almost orgasm on the spot. I can feel his erection straining against the confines of his clothes.

Grabbing the tent in his pants, he feels like a steel rod. I can only imagine what he looks like and how big he is because the strain in his pants is too much for me to know. I have to move my hand from him because my resolve is cracking. I can't have sex with this man. We have no protection! I know he's clean, I took his blood and recorded the results myself. But still, I'm not that kind of girl to screw a guy I just met with no condom. Add in that he is a damn cop, a crooked one at that, and I am not giving up the cookie for no protection.

Never once does he let go of my lips, his tongue assaulting mine, and I can't fight back the moan that escapes my lips. His hand is still tangled in my hair and he pulls a little more forcefully.

I can feel the wetness flooding out of me, coating my thighs in my arousal, and his free hand caresses my side, running a track to the sweet spot. Everywhere his fingertips have grazed feels like a fire has been set upon my skin. When he finally gets to my clit and touches that little bundle, I think I might explode. He trails his finger in a circle teasing my clit, and I am almost panting in anticipation. Every time he swipes my clit with his finger my legs jerk and I can't control my moans. Taking his hand from my hair he runs it along my jaw to my mouth. Once I get his middle finger close to my parted lips, I suck on it showing him my oral talents, and he groans. It's a husky sound and it seems to surprise him because his eyes close and his breathing gets heavy.

"Sweetass, you keep sucking on my finger like that, showing off your talents then you are gonna have to put them pretty lips on my cock."

I look him straight in his mesmerizing blue eyes and suck as hard as I can with all my might. As soon as I do that, he plunges two fingers into me. Letting go of his finger, I come with a scream, I feel heat from the top of my head to the tips of my curled toes and it is delicious. I never want to stop this feeling of him being inside of me, of being so completely full of him, even if it is just his fingers. I forget about our conditions and our surroundings, so when he clamps his hand over my mouth, it startles me and pulls me out of my state. Looking at him with big, wide eyes he can see that he scared me.

"You are being too loud, Sweetass, someone might hear us, and I certainly don't want to share this body with anyone else, but I will die tryin' before anyone does."

I don't know if his words scare me more or not. I guess I will never know because once his fingers start moving in me again all fear is gone. I want this man like I have never wanted anything before. Maybe my decisions are from being sex starved for as long as I have, but I find myself using my feet to pull his pants down. Inmates wear scrubs just like us nurses, so I know I could hook my toes and work them down. I just have to feel him and condom or not, I will feel him. Stupid decisions are made sometimes in the heat of the moment. Hopefully this isn't the dumbest decision in the history of my decisions.

His dick springs free with a bob like it's on a spring. Wrapping my hand around it, I realize that he has moved his body so he can keep two fingers in me and still play with my clit while I grab his cock. I can barely get my fingers to touch he is so huge. Hearing his groans just turns me on even more. I need to taste him. Flipping myself around, before he can protest, my mouth is on him. Salty and smooth, he seems to get impossibly harder in my mouth. Hissing through his teeth, he grabs ahold of my hair as if it were an anchor and I'm the only thing keeping him on the ground. The push and pull of my mouth and the soft velvety feel of him has me ready to orgasm again. He leaves me in a constant state of lust that I never knew was possible between two people.

"Fuck, Livvy, I can't even begin to describe how your mouth feels like a slice of heaven. When we get the fuck out of here, I am going to claim your mouth and your pussy. You won't be able to move once I am done with you. Fuck, I won't be able to move. This is the type of mouth that can move mountains, and I cannot wait to take advantage of it."

Shivering at his words, he thrusts even further down my throat. Gagging, I relax myself to open up more before the tears spring to my eyes. I reach down massaging my clit, trying to find some kind of relief for the pressure that is building within me. As soon as my finger touches my clit, I feel like I could blow.

"Stop. Stop fucking touching yourself, and stop sucking my cock. I refuse to blow it in your mouth. I will blow it when your pussy is strangling my cock, but only after I leave you a sweating, sobbing mess from all of the fucking orgasms I give you. So, Sweetass, stop."

Oh God, I can't take it anymore, and I say the one thing I will probably regret, but still, I can't help it. "Just fuck me." Like I said before, in the heat of the moment, dumb decision are made. It has been too long since I have had sex and even longer since I have had good sex.

He looks like he is battling some internal war, and I wonder which Damian is going to win. "Are you sure?" is all he says to me. Nodding at him, I see the relief in his eyes, I guess he was having a hard time holding back as well.

"This is going to be quick, not because I can't handle being inside your pussy, but because we need to find a way to get the fuck out of here, so eventually I can take my time cherishing this pussy like it should be."

Looking into my eyes he sees right through me like he can see every secret, every scar left by another person. He can see everything. He leans down and steals my breath away in a blazing hot kiss that curls my toes, then I feel the plump head of his dick at my entrance. He looks me in the eyes one last time before plunging in and taking what he wants. As he thrusts in and out of me, I can feel the sweat forming a light sheen on my body. The smell of sex permeates the air, making me forget that we are in the middle of a riot and that he is a crooked cop. All I can hear are my moans and the slapping of skin on skin. All I can feel is pure ecstasy that I have never felt before, not even with Jack's dad. It's as if my body was made for this moment. My body was made to take him, but what happens when things go back to normal and I need to let him go?

Damian is on his knees and he lifts me at the waist so I am kind of laying at an angle. Just having his hands on me makes me want to orgasm. I know without a doubt that this will be the orgasm to end all orgasms. This will be the end of me, I will lose myself completely. I'm close, but I can't quite reach it, and I don't know why. It's in my mind, but I can't quite grasp it.

"Come for me, sweetass," he groans out each word, grinding into me as he says it, and I lose it. My body knew what it needed, it needed to hear that smooth, sinful voice.

Holding me still, I know that he is coming too. I have to clap a hand over my mouth so that I don't draw attention to ourselves with my screams. My climax hits hot and heavy, with me raking my nails down his chest and makes me go numb. My battery operated boyfriend has never made me come like this. Even with Jack's dad, it was nothing compared to this, just like I knew it would be. This is the type of fuck that a girl tears up on, but won't because nobody wants a crying girl after sex. But the emotion of the situation we are in is almost too much.

DAMIAN

Holy shit! Never, have I ever felt pussy like that. Her pussy fit around my cock like a glove, and when she came, I thought she would snap my dick off with how tight her pussy contracted. It's every guy's dream to find the pussy that is made for you. Well, I fucking found it, and now it's all I can think about to get it again. Now that I have had her bareback, there will never be another time of wearing a condom with this chick again. It's funny because here would be the time for the awkwardness to set in after giving it good to a girl, you know, when you are trying to get dressed and split. I feel none of that. I do, however, try to get dressed because I need to tell her my plan and for me to tell her the truth.

I make quick work of getting my pants back on when I hear the loudspeaker come on again.

"Oh, Olivia, you sound so sweet when you come, I can't wait to have you scream when I shove my cock down your throat. I heard you suck a mean cock. You have little time left before I start slitting your friend's throats. I'm giving you one more chance to come to me, if not, then you can have their deaths on your conscience. I wonder who I will start with first, Mary? What about the beautiful Cori, I'm sure she wants my cock shoved in her while I slit her throat? The warden? Ahhh, yes, I can see your face, I can see the lightbulb shining. You didn't think I had them all? Come on, Olivia, I didn't get to the top by not being smart. Now get your bitch ass over here before I start slitting throats and bathing in their blood."

Her eyes fade from brown to black as the will to fight visibly leaves her. She looks absolutely defeated while I am absolutely enraged. That bastard saw us fucking. I don't know what makes me insane more, the fact that he is threatening her or that he saw her come. I am going to go with both. This fucker will pay the ultimate price, and I will personally send his ass to Hell.

"Do not feed into him. Do not give him what he wants, Livvy," I say with a slight plea in my voice. I don't want this to break her. I won't let this break her. She just nods and finishes getting dressed. She won't look me in the eye. That worries me because throughout the short time that I have known her, she has always looked everyone in the eyes. Even when Xavier did the fucked up shit he did to her, she still stared straight at him when she hit him.

"Livvy, I need to find a place for you to stay so that I can go to him. I will get you home safe to your kid. If I find somewhere safe for you to go will you promise you will stay there?" Shit. She has her knees pulled to her chest and she is just blankly staring around. I talk to her as if she is a child, because I feel one wrong move and she will bolt and go on a suicide mission to him.

I wrap her in my arms and let her fall apart. She cries into my chest and I hope that as she does, the burdens are easing. I can carry a lot more of the load than she is giving me, but she doesn't know me well enough to understand that. Giving her a few minutes to fall apart, I look around for cameras. I need to get her to the broom closet I had found earlier when I was getting food. But I cannot risk him seeing me leave her somewhere and then see me walking around alone. So I need to find a way to take the cameras out on this block without it appearing to be obvious.

With a heaving sigh and the crying hiccups, she seems done. Looking into her beautiful brown eyes, the eyes that could start wars, I have no choice but to kiss her. She still has that hiccup that girls get when they cry, but she kisses me back feather light, like whispers being told from her lips. I need to break away from her because she is making me feel some kind of way, and with what I do and the way I lead my life, I can't catch feelings for this girl. She certainly shouldn't catch feelings for me. Like a lead weight, my past comes down on me forcing me to break the kiss, the kiss that I want to hold onto forever.

With a little more gruffness in my voice, I tell her to come on. She seems to sense my change and gives me a wide-eyed stare like I kicked a puppy in front of her. I hate seeing the light dimming from her eyes so I turn to walk out of the room, not even waiting for her to follow. I just need a moment to breathe, because ever since I met this tiny girl she has invaded every sense and every brain cell I ever had. She's like a daydream and a nightmare altogether. Sweet and innocent but with a terrible ending. That ending hasn't happened yet, but it will once I get her home safe and sound to her kid and I am still sitting in this shithole.

Making my way down the hall, I think of how to do this with the cameras not seeing her. But right now, I don't think I have any other choice, she has just got to go in and wait.

"Right here, stay in here and don't come ouwt until the cops come get you."

Without a passing glance, she walks into the closet and that's it. I wish I had a better plan, but there aren't many options in this place, so I have to work with what little resources I have. With what feels like a slam to my heart, I shut the door to the closet and lock the door with the guard's keys I lifted earlier. My only saving grace is that I do have the keys, so it gives Olivia more time to prepare if someone tries to break in.

Making the long walk down the hall, I remember the two idiots I messed up and that I need to get cuffs to restrain them with. Burton's body is still lying on the ground, a burnt putrid smell hanging in the air from where he lays. Searching his body for cuffs is taking so much out of me. I want to vomit because the smell of burnt flesh has never been my strong suit. Finding two pairs of cuffs, I make my way into the cell and see that only one is still conscious.

"He's going to gut you like a fucking fish," he slurs out as he wheezes a pained laugh and his face winces.

"He already knows where she lives, her routines, what her kid looks like, her mom. He even knows that her dad's dead and where she went to school. He knows everything about her. Once you're rotting away, he is going to punish her."

My blood runs cold. I knew Xavier had a far reach, but I didn't know how far. He must have someone in law enforcement on his payroll to run that extensive of a background check. If I fail, if I fucking die, he will destroy her whole family. I can't fail at this because I won't let that happen. With an iron fist I know the bastard out, sick of hearing the shit he's spewing. None of it matters anyways, I have heard enough to know that this is bigger than just her. I have to save not only her but her family, too. Not to mention the people that X already has.

I allow fear to take over for a few minutes before I make my way toward where X is. The what if's are running through my mind about a million miles a minute.

I have never had so many people depend on me. People that don't even know they are relying on me, are in fact banking on me to actually pull this off. My hands shakes and my breathing labors, and I realize that I am about to have a panic attack. I've never had one before, but I recognize the signs. Sitting down, I take a moment to gather myself. I take a deep breath and send up a silent prayer. As I stand to my feet, I notice the camera in the corner. Drawing my hand up, I aim two fingers toward the lens and mimic shooting a gun.

I walk out into the dark of night, and I'm instantly on high alert. I know Xavier is fully in control of the prison, sitting in the control room like a king on his throne. The late spring air is warm and muggy, but humid like water clinging to your skin. I instantly break out into a sweat as if I've have been exerting myself for hours.

I know where I'm going because the building is lit up like a fucking Christmas tree. I can hear men groaning, some yelling, and some crying. Seems like a battlefield out here, with death and destruction permeating the air. Slowly easing my way towards where the devil hides, the coast seems to be clear. I stumble over a body, I don't know if it was inmate or guard, but I have to right myself so I don't fall on my face.

As I enter the building, I remind myself I have no plan. The element of surprise went out the window a long time ago. I have zero weapons on me, so I am going in completely unprotected. Hopefully my wits will be enough.

Olivia

I have a sinking feeling like I am drowning in just a puddle. Lives are potentially being lost as I sit here in the dark trying not to make a sound. But even though I am not making any noise on the outside, my insides are screaming and throwing a fit. My heart is aching with the feelings of loss, and I can't help but think about Cori and Mary. They both have been so good to me since I have been here, and I can't help but feeling like this is all my fault. I am responsible for anything that happens to them.

I can feel my breathing coming on faster, I am sweating profusely and I know that I am in the midst of a panic attack. This is all on me, all my fault. Those words just keep repeating in my head. If I had never hit Xavier that first time, all of this would be avoided. He wouldn't be fixated on me, he wouldn't have done this. Damian's words replay in my head reminding me that Xavier is extremely dangerous, rapes and mutilates women. The panic is worse. The darkness is closing in. We all fear the monsters under our beds, but Xavier has proven that it is people that go bump in the night. I can handle a monster, a crazy maniac hell bent on revenge is something I can't handle. But I have to, there is no other choice in the matter. I have to do something. Sitting here in the dark is not good for my sanity when God knows what is going on. All I'm picturing is death and destruction and me sitting smack dab in the middle of it.

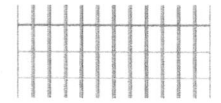

I start in a panic, screaming and thrashing about in the small space. Taking in my surroundings I realize I must have dozed off while trying to clear my thoughts. I was in the midst of my worst nightmare. My sweet Jack staring back at me with lifeless eyes. My mother, taking her last gurgling breaths. The terror I felt in that nightmare is still stinging my heart. Making my breathing come in rapid, shallow breaths.

"Get your shit together, Olivia. Can't help if you are freaking out," I chastise myself out loud, and then mentally kick myself because

Damian tried drilling into my head before he left that I needed to be quiet. I need to not draw attention to myself. My mind is running a million miles a minute, and I feel as if the walls are closing in. What do I do? What if someone has heard me and is just waiting for me to peek my head out of the door? So many questions with no answers. What if Damian fails and I am just sitting here, waiting on X to kill me? I need to peek, I need to crack this door to see if anyone is waiting for me. I think that will be the only thing to ease my mind and stop this slow crawl into a panic attack before these walls cave in on me, and I truly start freaking out.

Wiping my sweaty palms on my pants, my hands shake as I reach for the cold door knob. Turning it, it doesn't open! Then I remember that there is a deadbolt and I need to unlock the door before it opens. Typical, even in a crisis, I am a fumbling idiot. Turning the lock over, it clicks loudly and I am sure someone hears me. On bated breath, I twist the cold metal in my hand, and open the door just a fraction and look straight ahead into nothing. The power has been out on the block and so the only thing on is every few lights are on dim, meaning the auxiliary lights have kicked on.

Opening the door a little more, I know it's a good sign that the corridor is empty. It means Xavier hasn't sent for me yet, but it's only just a matter of time. He won't stop until he gets me, I know that, but maybe I could sneak attack on him while Damian is trying to get him as well? He is expecting Damian to try to rescue me, but hell, I am a strong woman. I don't need a man to come to my rescue, I need to save myself and my friends! Girl power and all that shit. Now I just need to come up with a plan for not getting myself killed.

DAMIAN

Opening the door to the main control building feels like I am walking into Hell's gate. It takes every ounce of strength I can muster to pull the handle and walk inside as the smell of my death lurks at my feet. I have so many people relying on me to get them out, most importantly Olivia. My sweet, beautiful and sassy girl. She doesn't even realize the hold she has on me in this short amount of time. It certainly isn't love yet, but getting out of this shit hole, getting away from the drama, I could certainly see this turning into love. I've never loved anyone before. The thought scares the shit out of me, more than walking into this lion's den.

I need to clear these thoughts before I walk inside! I cannot go in here acting like some love sick fool! He will see right through me and kill me right away. I need to give Xavier the illusion that was just in it to fuck her, and now I am delivering her in a locked closet, just for him. As far as his buddies that are still handcuffed and knocked out in the cell? I guess I need to come up with an explanation for them quick.

The place is lit up like a Christmas tree, especially with all the lights out throughout the rest of the prison. I can still hear that pained moaning sound, and the further I walk the louder the agonizing sound gets. I scan each room as I pass by to ensure they are clear of anyone, then I keep walking into what feels like the belly of the beast.

After clearing what looks like someone's office, I can tell that whoever is moaning is in the next room, and I try to prepare myself. Peering into the long glass window on the door, it's not the office break room that catches my attention, but the girl tied to a chair that has since fallen over with the girl lying on her side. What turns my stomach and almost makes me lose its contents is her face. A jagged X is carved into her face with the ends beginning at her temples, crossing over her nose and ending at the corner of her jaw line. Although the wound is obviously fresh, the bleeding appears to have stopped. She seems to be passed out but still moaning in her sleep like her body is still awake. As much as it pains me, I need to keep moving. I know she is alive, and leaving her there is safer.

Since nobody is in the room with her that means that they have left her for dead, and leaving her is her best hope for survival. I can't tell if this is Cori or Mary, but given the fact that she is wearing dirty scrubs, I know she works with Olivia.

Rounding the corner, I see him. Sitting at one of the visitation tables almost like an official person, around him are men with probably a sick case of hero worship. Cons are all the same, they stick together, and they will always be that way. These guys are all the ones who are with Xavier, definitely not a snitch in this bunch. If you are a snitch, of course, you know the saying "snitches get stitches." More like snitches go in ditches. Snitches die all the time in prison, which is I'm sure accounting for the dead men around him.

Xavier's guys drag in another guy having him kneel before Xavier like some king on a throne, this guy is already beaten to a pulp, and his face is nearly unrecognizable. I can't make out what Xavier says to him, but I see X raise his foot and kick the guy in the face, he lands in a heap at X's feet. The guys drag him off and throw him on top of a guard that has already been killed. But I also see an older woman, eyes open, unseeing. She isn't wearing any pants, and like the girl down the hall, there is an X carved into her face. Although, this bitch's throat has been slit, a thick pool of blood kissing the floor. I don't know how long she has been dead, but it seems like she died a horrible, painful death. I am assuming that this is Mary, although I am not sure. I hear moaning coming from a corner that I can't see yet since I haven't entered the room. Taking a deep breath, I walk in.

Olivia

Leaving that closet is the hardest thing I have ever had to do. When going somewhere I don't want to go, I find that my feet feel like concrete and putting one foot in front of the other seems near impossible. The only thing that is keeping me moving is thoughts of my friends and Jack. If it wasn't for them, I probably would just lay down and take whatever may come. I decide not to take the direct route to where Xavier is hiding. I want to go around and see what is out there. See if I can see any cops around the gates and fencing. I think that would make me feel better to see a brigade of rescue. Plus, it might give me the element of surprise if he doesn't see me leaving the direct path to where he is if he is watching the camera feeds.

Walking outside, I don't know what to expect, but pitch black is not what I was thinking I would see. It's completely dark, the shot tower lights aren't on which is usually a beacon of light. Shivers race up and down my spine, with goosebumps breaking out on my body. People never think they are afraid of the dark until they are in the pitch dark, and then you feel all kinds of things, from being watched to a deep despair of being alone. Let me say this now if a zombie apocalypse happened, I want at least one other person with me, so I wouldn't feel this lonely.

Rounding the corner, I see zero lights except the one building that I know Xavier is in. Makes me wonder where the cops are, they have to know by now. I mean seriously, I know my mom would have called 911 since I'm not home yet. Walking closer to the control room, it feels like a weight is holding me down, making it impossible to move.

The stillness of the night leaves a void of all sound, except the slight chirping from crickets and grasshoppers. The quiet chirps ring loud in my ears and I guess I'm hyper-aware to my surroundings. Nothing else is heard. I would think that there would be chaos outside with the fact that we are in the midst of a riot. I am assuming that most of the inmates have escaped.

Tip-toeing towards the building that very well could house the man that will destroy me, my mouth goes dry and the sweat factor increases tenfold. I hear the faint sounds of footsteps shuffling on concrete and I instantly freeze, and try to assess my surroundings, which is incredibly hard in the pitch black. Not hearing any other sounds and after controlling my breathing I continue on. Trying to keep my steps light I am almost to the control room when I can feel it. That tingling in your spine, the way the back of your head feels heavy because someone is near and they are watching. Before I can let out a scream, a big hand covers my mouth and pulls me to the ground. The last thing I see is a fist coming straight for my face before it all goes black.

DAMIAN

"I didn't think your dumb ass would come to us. I was letting you enjoy the last piece of pussy you were ever going to have before I rip your heart out," Xavier snarls.

"Yeah, well, she's got a grade A piece of pussy, once you get it, you don't know what to do with yourself. How I ended up here."

"See, Damian, I didn't want to kill you, I thought when we first got here that you would be an asset to me. But you kept watching her whenever she came near, then I knew you were stuck on the smell of her pussy, so you would never be with me, just against me."

"You didn't know that, Xavier, you carried this out with the help of your wannabes, and you never knew what I could do for you," I bite out, knowing he is falling into what I am saying.

"And what is that? What could you do for me that I can't do myself?"

"Take you straight to her." He looks shocked. Good, it's what I wanted. He licks his nasty lips, and I want nothing more than to pull them off with my bare hands. But I need him to trust me.

"Xavier, not only can I take you straight to her, but I can tell you everything about the bitch."

"Ahhh, I see. Am I supposed to believe that you aren't trying to save her?" I can see the evil glint in his eye.

"You can believe whatever the fuck you want to believe, but pussy is pussy. I've had my fill, so now I don't care what you do to her. Just had to get my dick wet before you got her."

"Don't blame you for wanting to get your dick wet, she is a fine piece of pussy. But my question to you is, you're an ex-cop so how the fuck am I supposed to believe that you don't have some sort of hero complex and want to save her?"

"Are you done? I'll go get her right now, but I don't have to explain myself to you." I turn on my heel to walk out keeping my ears open for any movement behind me. I guess I am so distracted by making sure he doesn't make a move on me that I didn't see some big guy bring in an unconscious Olivia thrown over his shoulder.

"Yes, the main guest has arrived at our little party. Now tell me, dirty cop, what is saving me from gutting you like a fish? What are you going to do now that I have no need for you? You're a dirty cop which let's face it, are a dime a dozen in this city. I have plenty on my payroll, I don't need one that has already been caught being dirty and landed in this shit hole."

As Xavier speaks, I find it amusing that he is the leader of a gang. He has a way of talking that people just respond to. It's hard to think he has done the ruthless shit that he has. You almost feel like you are listening to a Mafia boss instead of a street gang leader.

The brute that has Olivia dumps her on the floor which causes her to stir. I notice a little swelling by her eye and my blood boils. But there is nothing I can do about it.

Xavier looks at her like she is a prized show pony as she writhes around on the floor, moaning in pain. He licks his lips sinisterly like the Big Bad Wolf. When he looks up at me and smiles I know this isn't going to be good.

"I want you to bring me her mom and son."

Olivia

Ouch, my eye hurts! And for the love of all that is talking, whoever is talking, please shut the fuck up! I think to myself. I'd voice it all out loud, but it feels like I can't open my mouth. Cotton seems to have replaced the saliva in my mouth and I would give anything for water. Everything is a blur. I was walking through the pitch black corridor when suddenly the darkness became *darker*. It's funny how you can't remember what happened and then all of a sudden you do and it hits you like a ton of bricks. You get paralyzed and rooted to where you lay when either the fear or embarrassment hit you. This time I'm not embarrassed, I'm scared out of my wits. Keeping my eyes closed because I don't want to face the man that will end my life.

Hearing the voices a little more clearly, I can pick out that smooth as raw silk on your skin, sweet as honey voice of Damian. I think I could pick that voice up anywhere. But I also hear him. The slick tongue of Xavier, like a snake in the grass slithering his words over my skin. Goosebumps break out, my fight or flight is screaming at me to get up and run, but I'm paralyzed. The fear is too much, I just want to lay here.

Then I hear Xavier say words that instantly has my blood running cold, shoving ice right through my veins. He wants Damian to go get Jack and my mom. I can't let them get hurt. I will fight to the death if I have to, and I will win because nobody and I mean nobody will hurt my son. I realize that I am waiting with bated breath for what Damian will say.

"Why, Xavier?"

"Because what better way to get this bitch whore to do what I want? She can watch me tear her boy apart limb from limb. She can listen to him scream out for her and watch as his life drains before her eyes," he snarls.

"I'll do what I can, but I make no promises Xavier. How the hell do you expect me to not get caught?"

"I don't give a good goddamn how you expect to not get caught. Just get me the fucking boy and mother. Use your cop connections, I know most are just as dirty as you. I employ most of the dirty ones who are filthier than me."

"Say I do this, say I get the kid and the mom, what the hell then?" Damian is a fucking rat, I knew it. I wanted to trust him so bad.

"Then we talk about your employment opportunities," Xavier says it so nonchalantly, as a business man in some corporate tower giving out his dinner order.

I'm scared. Terrified. No. No, there are no words to convey just how terrified I am. But I know this, I know that I will not let this monster hurt my baby. I don't care if he rips me limb by limb, having a world where my baby boy is gone is a world I don't want to live in. It's a world I won't live in. In my short time on this earth, his is even shorter. He has such a bright light about him, and I refuse to let it get snuffed out by some maniac.

Rolling onto my side I start coughing. My stomach hurts like someone stepped on me. Standing up hurts, but I manage to get my feet under me. I don't know what I am going to do when I see Xavier but gouge his eyes out is a good option.

"Finally, the bitch has woken up." Nope, not his eyes, I want to rip his tongue out with my bare hands. I spit by his feet.

"Damian, before you leave, hold her. She needs to learn a fucking lesson." The urge to go limp in Damian's arms is strong, but I need to stand my ground.

"You don't have a lesson that I need to learn." Sassy, but will probably be costly.

"Oh bitch, I am going to enjoy this. Damian, take her to her knees."

Xavier unties the drawstring on his pants, and I immediately freeze. Damian wraps his hands around my arms and lifts as if he is going to carry me to the enemy. Which I guess in a sense he is.

"Olivia, just do as you are fucking told. Maybe he will let you live" Damian says, and Xavier immediately starts laughing this deep, throaty sound that makes my skin crawl.

"Let her live? I wouldn't let her live if it was down to her or the cop that arrested me. Poor, poor Olivia. So scared, so sweet. I can't wait to taste your life as it flows out of you. You will be punished for all the things you have done to me. I am going to keep you alive for as long as I can. I want you to see what I do to your boy, so you can't miss that show now, not when you are the main star!"

It's funny how you lose all hope because something weird happens. A feeling of fullness fills you, almost like you can't take anymore so your body shuts off. You kind of tune out what people say, it is like your body is saying, 'it's ok, I got you.'

"Olivia, just go. I mean shit, you wanted to suck my cock the minute you met me. I'm sure you know how and I am sure you will be fine," Damian says to me, his words filling me with the sour taste of disgust. I rear my head back to head butt him, but I miss. If I get out of this shit storm, I will murder him with my bare hands. I never thought I would be capable of murder, I was too pure to do something so evil. But right now, I could and would do it, if it changed the situation.

Damian shoves me towards Xavier, and I start to dry heave. I want to vomit, but nothing will come up. These heaves sound like they come from the bottom of my feet all the way up. I can't do this, I just can't. Just thinking of that man putting his dick anywhere near my mouth has me finally emptying the contents of my stomach down on my shoes. Damian drops me, and I fall to all fours while still heaving.

"You nasty bitch! It's ok you don't have to suck my cock, for now. But I will get a piece then."

He slowly starts to walk toward me, and it's as if I can see the air moving with each of his steps. The heaving hasn't stopped, just nothing is coming out anymore and I am a sweaty mess. He starts to rub his erection through his pants and using his other hand to untie the drawstring on his pants. This is it, this is the end.

I feel so betrayed by Damian. When we were alone, he was all 'I won't let anything happen to you, Livvy.' The revelation of his betrayal hits me like a slap in the face with ice cold water. He is trying to tell me something. I don't know what it is, but he has never called me Olivia by choice before, only when I yell at him over it. It's always been Livvy.

DAMIAN

Watching Xavier stalk toward my woman is the hardest thing I have ever had to do. Not even when I was first sentenced to prison and had no idea what to expect of life behind the gate did that moment compare to the helplessness I feel now. She is completely cracked and rightfully so. I have betrayed her. I am trying to get a message to her, but she is too zoned out to comprehend anything. Now she is on the floor with this piece of shit walking towards her.

"Wait. What if I get her ready for you?" I implore, trying to keep the plea out of my voice.

"Why should I let you?"

"Because I have been in this pussy, so I know it's good. You want her all ready for you don't you? I can make her go limp, and turn to putty in your hands." I feel sick.

"Okay, yeah, she needs to be ready for this dick. Possibly all the other dicks in here too."

I walk over to where she is still spewing on the floor. Even a sweaty, pukey mess she is still the most beautiful, breathtaking creature I have ever seen. I want nothing more than to grab her and run like hell, only stopping for her kid and Mom. I go to push some hair from her face, and she smacks my hand away. I deserve it even if I don't like it. She hates me and rightfully so, but it doesn't hurt any less. But it shows me that she still has fight left in her. Thank God.

"Olivia."

"Don't you fucking touch me, don't you dare touch me! You hurt me, you have been working with him, and I said it when all this started, but you promised me! You fucking promised!" her voice is loud, deep from within her lungs and tears cascade like a waterfall down her face. I wish I could take the betrayal away, but maybe this is for the better.

"Olivia, look at me. I said look at me dammit!"

Finally, her eyes reach mine. Bloodshot and swollen, but still beautiful. I haven't quite figured out how I am going to play this out. I mean Xavier is a seriously sick fuck for thinking that I am going to get a woman primed for him, let alone my woman. She doesn't know it yet, but she is mine. Since the moment transport brought us all in, seeing her in that clinic, she took up residence in my head and hasn't stopped since.

Once I finally have her eyes on mine, I wink at her to try to calm her and let her know that I got this. Even though I don't. I feel like the room has gone up ten degrees, it's fucking sweltering in here. Looking around, there are at least five guys that I can see present in the room in addition to Xavier. Not good odds when a weapon is nowhere in sight. Wiping my brow, Xavier paces behind me. Guess I am not moving fast enough for his liking. Too fucking bad, the piece of shit can wait on me.

"Olivia, baby, it will all be alright. I promised you before," I coo in the most soothing voice I have. Used to be one that got the ladies to drop their panties for me.

"Fuck off, Damian, you lied to me. Now you are doing his dirty work! I can't believe I ever thought we might have stood a chance. I can't believe that I trusted that you would take care of me, keep me safe, and keep my son safe! You are no better than him."

Ouch, she truly believes that I would betray her like that. I would think she would realize that I am trying to stall and buy us some time. Xavier laughs uncontrollably, and I want nothing more than to rip the smugness off of his face.

"You actually thought that he was going to save you? You actually thought that you stood a chance, or that he wasn't working for me? You are dumber than I thought, bitch! He has been working for me for a little while now! He's dirty, that's how he landed in this shithole in the first place. Once a dirty cop, always a dirty cop! He played you, just like I thought he would. First chance to give you up and he took it."

If she wasn't defeated before, she certainly is now. It is like watching a train wreck, you can see how the words are registering in her mind, and you can see the light go out. She is done, she has surrendered, and now I am fucked.

Olivia

So there is my confirmation. He has been in on it, even though I was hoping he wasn't. He got me to believe him and I fell hook, line, and sinker all the way to this black abyss that has consumed me. Honestly, the fight or flight has left me and all that remains is despair. My Jack, my beautiful baby boy. That is the little beacon of hope that I have. His face in my mind's eye is the only thing that is bringing me some solace that everything will end up well.

Sitting up now, I try to take in my surroundings. A few guys hanging around with the same prurient expression as Xavier. All look like dogs that are about to have a final meal. It's a sickening feeling that sinks to the pit of your stomach knowing that the end is coming soon, and the end will be painful. I can only send an unspoken prayer to up above that this isn't as painful as I feel it will be.

Xavier advances towards me, walking with the grace and litheness of a cat. He tries to soften his features, making the lust and need not as apparent. Maybe in some ways he is trying to comfort me or ease my panic. I doubt that. Chances are he thrives on the shivers of fear that someone has towards him. He kneels down and sweeps some stray hair from my face.

Grabbing my chin and forcing me to look at him, he puts on his best soothing voice. "Shhh, Olivia, there is nothing you can do. You're stuck. Done and over with. I will enjoy ripping you limb from limb, I can't wait to hear you beg me to end you. When you hit me that first time, you signed and sealed your death. No cunt puts her hands on me without paying the price. Now, let us get started because I am not a patient man, and I have given you long enough. Now take off your goddamn clothes."

Reaching down to the bottom of my scrub shirt I feel the pre-loaded needles that I forgot I had. It offers a small modicum of comfort that I need. Pulling the shirt over my head, I am careful to hold the scrub pockets to keep the shots inside so don't tumble to the floor. I immediately cover myself even though I am wearing a bra.

"Take the rest of the shit off," Xavier snarls at me and spits in my direction.

Damian stands by Xavier, and I can see the muscles in his jaw ticking and a vein popping out of his neck. He is an odd shade of red, but his eyes never leave me. I stand my ground and don't move a muscle, I just continue to look at Damian and try to cover myself up.

The smack to my cheek comes out of nowhere from one of Xavier's lackey's, and I am instantly on the ground. The heat from the hit has my face feeling like it is on fire with pain blossoming around my eye. Before I can truly get my bearings, I feel hands all over me, pushing and pulling at the scraps of fabric that were covering me. Crying out I try to fight back, but I'm met with another smack to the face. This time, blood fills my mouth and the copper taste makes me want to heave again. As I turn my head to the side to spit the blood out, someone heavy straddles me, forcing my hands above my head.

Screaming, I start thrashing about trying to buck this guy off of me. My fight makes me feel super human as my adrenaline as my adrenaline soars through my veins. I will not go down without a fight now. I buck my hips up one good time and the guy goes flying. A stroke of good luck gets me because when I bucked him off he was still holding onto my arms so he didn't prepare to hit face first on the floor. He falls forward with a sickening crunch. No clue whether he is breathing, and personally I don't care right now, but either way he is knocked out cold.

Xavier shouts at two other men to get men, three if you include Damian. The two scramble to grab me and strip off my clothes. When you have hands grabbing, twisting, and pulling it is a sickening feeling. Hopelessness and despair fill you, you feel more alone than ever. As I lie there, now down to my bra and panties, I close my eyes and wave the proverbial white flag and surrender. There is nothing more that I can do to fight for myself and my family.

Closing my eyes in the hopes of not having to look any of these savages in the face, I feel a pain radiate down my side, but strangely the weight that was pinning me to the floor is gone. Instead, I hear grunting and the sound of flesh hitting flesh. Opening my eyes, it takes a second to focus which probably means I have a concussion from the hits to the face I have taken. Damian is fighting the two men as Xavier stalks toward me. Without reservation, I instantly get to my feet. I have hit him before and I will hit him again.

I rush towards my discarded scrub top and find the needles full of morphine. The blood is rushing to my ears, and I feel the adrenaline coursing through my veins. I palm the injection just as he tackles me against the floor. The needle tumbles out of my hand with a clatter to the floor. Xavier shoves his pants down then straddles me, struggling to get my panties down. He rips them away in one loud rip. He palms his dick, which is thin with a small, angry head. Scrambling to think of what to do next, I finally get a plan together in my head. It's quick and hopefully it will work.

DAMIAN

These assholes are relentless. I duck and dive trying to get these guys out of my way. Blood mixed with sweat is pouring down my face, pooling in the corners of my eyes. But I will continue to fight, for her. She is more than worth it, even with the hate in her eyes every time she looks at me. Knowing she is still breathing in this world, then I have done my job. If I fail and Xavier gets her in his clutches, I cannot imagine how the world will go on turning. My world definitely won't.

I see Olivia get to her feet and rush over to her shirt, start digging through the pockets on the front. What the fuck is she doing?

Xavier bum rushes her from her side before I can scream her name. Wouldn't have mattered much because this big tank like man lands an uppercut straight to my jaw, I almost go down like a sack of potatoes. I know that if my ass hits the ground, it will be over. They will take me out in a heartbeat. The other fucker just stands behind the big fucker bouncing on the balls of his feet like a prized fighter. He hasn't thrown as many punches so I can't see his weak spot. But the big dude, he definitely has a weakness. Before he throws a punch he points the foot of the hand he will throw.

Trying to get my shit together I spit the mouth full of blood from the last punch right square into the chest of the big dude. My stupid gene is showing full out, but I don't care, I need him to get so angry that he becomes reckless.

Big dude just whips his massive shirt off and throws it to the side and grins at me. He has a split in his lip from where I busted him in the mouth, but that is about all the damage he has. His buddy, the fighter, has no damage to him because he hasn't joined in. I try not to take my eyes off of him, but out of the corner of my mind there is movement. I see Olivia flat on her back with Xavier over her being ripped out of her panties. She is trying to fight, but it seems futile.

Seeing that sends me into overdrive. I have to be able to get to her, I would never live with myself if something happens to her. Noticing my distraction, the big guy comes at me, charging like a bull to a matador. I plant my feet. Treating him like a bull to a matador I spin when he gets close, letting him run head-first into the cinderblock wall. With a thud, he goes down like a ton of bricks. One down, one more to go.

I don't dare glance over at Olivia as the fighter circles around me. I square up and follow his movements, waiting for his first move. Studying his movements, I watch for him to show his hand. He has a slow hook and that is the opening I have been waiting for. As his first swings out, I land a kick to his gut that knocks the air right out of his fucking lungs. Had to have broken a few ribs because he is gurgling and struggling for air on the ground. Straddling his chest, I land a punch to the face that has him sleeping on the floor.

Standing up a loud shriek fills the air, and rushing over to Olivia. I see Xavier laying on top of her at an awkward angle. She is crying profusely, but he isn't moving. My heart is ready to drop out of my butt because she is scared and shaking and I have no idea what is going on.

"Olivia, baby, please talk to me!" I implore.

Olivia

Numb, darkness, despair, and dazed. I guess that is all that I am right now. That and I cannot breathe because of the weight of this monster on top of me.

"Get him off! Get him off of me NOW!" Panic is an understatement, I am full on close to hyperventilating. Sweat and blood pour down my face. Damian rushes over to me practically yelling in my face to tell him what is going on. I open my mouth to speak, but no words come out. I'm naked with a dead naked man on top of me and I want to escape.

"Please, please, please get him off of me. I'm begging you, please just let me go. I can't do this, I can't do any of this. I just want Jack, I need my boy."

Damian rolls Xavier off of me, his eyes are still open, but they have no spark in them. Lifeless and gone. As soon as he is off of me I roll to my side, I don't want anyone seeing me this way. He at least has the good sense to take off his shirt and cover me with it. My crying and hyperventilating turn into full on hysterics, and I don't know when it will stop.

I know that I'm in shock and it will wear off, but I swear that I heard Damian pick up the phone. I swear I also heard him say something to the effect of being Officer Damian Shaw. But how can that be? He is a dirty cop, he isn't even on the force, and he is a fucking prisoner! It must be the lack of oxygen to my brain because I slowly lose consciousness, but I have so many questions.

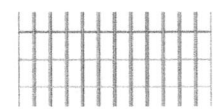

Beep Beep Beep

Ugh, rolling over I reach out to silence my alarm. But reaching out my arm I don't hit it where it normally is. Cracking an eye open I see that there is no nightstand and this is not my room. Sitting up with a start I immediately feel dizzy and lay back down.

"Hi sweetie, I'm Kimberly, your nurse. I know you must have a huge headache and I will tell you all about it, but there is someone who wants to see his mommy." She silences the alarm and goes to the door. Before she can get to it, Jack bursts through the door with my mother close behind.

He skids to a stop right before he reaches my bed, and I know he is scared. I hold my arms out and he instantly climbs up on the bed and into my arms. Squeezing him tight I look to my mom. She is in tears but trying not to let them fall.

"Are you ok?" My mom who is not normally an overly emotional woman is suddenly overwrought with tears.

"I'm ok, Mom. Just sore."

"Did he?" I know what she means, it makes me profoundly sad she has to ask.

"No, he didn't get a chance." The look of relief on her face crushes me. I should have never put her or my baby in this kind of situation in the first place.

"Momma, I was so scared. I thought I would never see you again. I tried so hard to help make grandma laugh while you were gone." He looks younger than his 8 years.

I squeeze him even harder. Never wanting to let him go again. "Damian kept me company when grandma was waiting for you to wake up."

That instantly stops me. I'm sure that I look like a fish out of water, opening and closing my mouth, trying to find the words. I send a look of confusion to my mom who is trying hard to gather her composure. She just smiles an all-knowing Mom smile at me.

Just then the doctor comes in to talk to me.

"Miss Ambrose, I'm Dr. Edwards, and I need to examine you now that you have woken up." Looking at my child in my arms and my mother he meekly asks them to step outside.

After going through the normal what is my name, how old am I, and general neuro exam he starts to look a little embarrassed so I am sure that his next set of questions will be uncomfortable.

"Miss Ambrose, we performed a rape kit on you when you were brought in, but I still have to ask if you were sexually assaulted," I don't know how this guy got his license because he is extremely shy and gets red-faced asking tough questions.

"No, he never got the chance, I," my voice trails off and tears spring to my eyes threatening to overflow. He just nods his head and continues on.

"You were very lucky to not have any breaks especially with the hits you took to the face. You do have a concussion along with losing consciousness so I am going to keep you at least another day for monitoring. Your face is bruised and you have a cut on your forehead and jaw that did not require stitches. You were very lucky. There is an officer here who would like to talk to you." Yeah, lucky me. I killed a man who was trying to rape me in the middle of a prison break.

As he leaves the room, I try to turn on my side but the soreness just won't let me without exerting myself too much. So I settle for turning my head, I didn't expect to see the cops so soon. When I turn around, I am greeted with a familiar pair of glacier blue eyes staring straight at me.

DAMIAN

Seeing her laying there is one of the most excruciating pains I have ever felt. Feels like someone took a rusty butter knife and carved out my heart. I am scared to walk any further for fear of how she will react to me.

"Why are you not in prison?" she asks with a resigned tone to her voice like she doesn't give a shit about me. I know she doesn't mean it. She can't mean it.

"Well, I never got to tell you what I needed to tell you. I wasn't a prisoner. I am part of the prison police system working undercover. It is a special unit that was designed to gain information from high profile inmates in the hopes of solving cold cases. I work for the state and have been to almost every prison in the state as an inmate. They recruited me to get Intel. I was in the system basically to watch over Xavier. To gain his trust so that maybe he would give up his crimes. I never meant to lie to you, but I had to. I'm so sorry. You never were a part of the plan. But when I saw you, I just knew that I would have to have you. I was supposed to get in, get info, and get transferred out. So far nobody has ever suspected that I was not a prisoner. Even the guards aren't privy to that info. Only the warden and my unit, and it would put a price on my head if anybody found out. I have been doing this for a while now and never once has this happened. Never once have I compromised my whole world for someone. I do my job and I do it well, but when you came along, all I could think about is you. You were everything from the first time I saw you. I tried to protect you since then"

She looks like she doesn't believe me. So I grab my badge out of my back pocket and toss it onto her bed. I can see her tentatively look at it like it will burn her if she touches it. The tears are swimming in her eyes, and I am sure that this is overwhelming to her. Hell with all that I'm feeling, it's overwhelming to me. She looks at the badge and then closes my wallet. It seems final. Like when she closed it, since she knows the truth is out she's done. But little does she know, I will bend over backwards for her forgiveness, I will slay dragons or bring her the stars if I have to. Because she is it for me. The end, I don't want anybody else. I want her and Jack.

I mean yeah it's sudden, and yeah it is probably too soon. But I guess when a person knows, they know. I used to never believe in love, used to fuck women from here to next week, a different name and a different face every day of the week. Now? Now it's all her and her son. That means I need to get my shit straight for them. I need to grow up and become the man that they need me to be.

"Say something," I plead.

She opens her mouth to speak but no words come out.

"I didn't mean to lie to you. You have to believe that. I tried to protect you, I tried to divert his fixation from you. But he started to get suspicious when I kept trying to get his sick mind off of you. So I had to back off, that was why I couldn't warn you when he went to smear the nut on your face mask. From then on, he lost all trust for me. I couldn't get close to him to find out that he was planning all of this to get to you. I would have killed him myself had I known."

I'm not ashamed to say that I would get on my knees and beg if she needs me to. This tiny woman has me all tied up in knots inside. On the one hand I want her and on the other I feel like it would be best to walk away and let her and her kid lead their lives away from me. That little devil on my shoulder thinks I should run and run fast. The angel on my shoulder is telling me that I can do this. I can be who she needs me to be.

She still has a look of disbelief but the tears have finally tripped over the ledge and have made their way down her face. Taking a few more steps toward her I can see that she is shaking. Whether it be with anger or anxiety, I don't know. She hasn't said. Hell she has barely looked at me since I came in. She has mainly stared through me.

"Say something," I repeat my earlier words, hoping that maybe she will. I will wait until she says whatever is on her mind.

Five long minutes goes by while we are on a stare down. The only sound in the room being the sound of her IV pump.

"Say something!" I am being more forceful with my words now. She has to speak to me dammit. Because I can't walk out of this room not knowing if I am walking away forever.

This woman has the ability to destroy me. That realization while I am waiting on her to say something is like a kick in the gut. Never has anyone had this much power over me. I can't say that I hate it. Because sometimes we meet someone who is meant to be in our lives for a short time. But sometimes they stay forever. She is my forever, she is my home.

Olivia

Stunned and shocked does not even begin to describe what I'm feeling. I mean seriously, he couldn't have dropped a clue? I have nothing that I can say to him right now, so he continues on speaking, almost like he has verbal diarrhea because he cannot stand the silence between us.

"I met your son. He is exactly like you, headstrong and powerful. I think he had me wrapped around his pinkie the minute I met him. Your mom is great too. Livvy, please talk to me." His expression is that of desperation.

As soon as his nickname for me is out of my mouth something clicks. How could I have been so blind and stupid? I pride myself on being smart, I read mystery and romance, and I do crossword puzzles. I just can't believe I missed it.

"When he had me captured you called me Olivia. Were you trying to tell me something?"

"I was hoping you would have picked up on it and realized I wasn't working for him. I was trying to give you a signal of sorts, I guess it backfired."

"What about Cori, Mary and everyone else?"

He starts rubbing the top of his head. He has short hair so there is nothing for him to run his fingers through. I know whatever he says is going to be bad.

"Well, Cori is alive and in the ICU. I'm so sorry, but Mary and the Warden were killed. Seven other guards died. Josh was caught at his home and arrested. I don't think he even suspected that I was police. I am so sorry, Livvy baby." He starts walking toward me and I put a hand out to stop him.

"What is it that you need Damian? Or is your name not Damian?" I know I am being a little catty, but I believe I deserve it for him not telling me.

"No, it's Damian Shaw. I have been an officer for the past few years after I got out of the Army. I never expected to meet someone like you, especially having the job that I have. I can go away for a few months at a time, so I never let anyone get close. But you wormed your way into me. It's like you are woven from the same cloth that I am, that makes you fit perfectly by my side."

"What about Xavier?" Tears spring to my eyes and I have to take a deep breath so they don't spill over. I refuse to shed tears over that monster.

"Dead. When you injected him with the morphine, his respiratory system shut down. You did good, babe."

"I'm not your babe, never have been and never will be."

Looking straight at him, that cocky smirk appears and his eyes fill with heat. I have to clench my thighs together to quell the pressure that is building within me. My body wants this man, desperately, almost like it has a siren call straight to him. But my body is a traitor because my brain is screaming no, you can't want him. Now which one to listen to? He is a gorgeous man and maybe my body is betraying me because he is so hot. He is standing in front of me in black cargo pants and a black Henley with a gun hanging on his hip. He looks like an avenging angel swooping down. He is so beautiful it is hard to look at him.

"Livvy, you have been mine since the moment I saw you. I had you once, I will have you again and I will never let you go. Mark my words sweetheart, you are always going to be mine. I'm ready whenever you are. Don't worry your pretty little head, I will wait for you, I will wait as long as you need me to. Because a feeling like this doesn't come along for everyone, and I will be damned if I let it pass us up when we could be so good together."

I fight hard to keep myself from giving into him. But he is right, from the moment I saw him, I was his. Whether I wanted to be or not, I was willing to risk everything to be with him. Is what we are feeling love? I don't know, but I can't let the feelings pass me up. What if this is my happily ever after of a fucked up fairy tale?

"You met Jack?" I try to change the subject while I process all of this in my head.

"Oh yeah, he is such a good kid. He was telling me all about some game he plays, mine something. He tried showing me on his tablet. Said he was playing online with a friend, but it looked like 2 cartoons walking around aimlessly and building stuff just to tear it down. He is a smart kid, just like his momma. Your mom is wonderful when she is not a nervous wreck. When you were brought in, she met us here. She was yelling at everyone and trying to push her way to you. I think security was scared of her."

Just hearing his words about Jack has me warming to him even more. I just don't know what to do, I need time. I need to breathe without worry from anyone or anything. But I don't think I can let him go. I don't want to let him go. But can I just let him into my life, hell, into Jacks life? What if it doesn't work out? Jack would be devastated. What about his job? Can I accept him being gone for who knows how long or if he will return?

He either senses my internal struggle or he's smart and giving me time. With a peck on the forehead, he tells me to rest and that he will be back in a bit.

Lying in this hospital listening to the hustle and bustle of the nurses makes me think of what am I going to do with my life. I certainly can't walk into that prison again, nor do I want to. I can't put my baby in jeopardy again. Pushing the call button, the nurse, I think her name is Kimberly comes in.

"Did you need something, hon?"

"Yes, how long was I asleep?

"Oh, you were asleep for 2 days, that sweet boy of yours was here a lot and that yummy man of yours was here every day and night. He only left when your mom and baby would come or if we needed to do something. You got lucky with that one. He is definitely one of the good ones, he had to get held down when the docs were trying to examine him because he didn't want to leave your sight. Screamed bloody murder to get to you!"

I'm surprised. Not because Jack was with me, but because Damian stayed and threw a temper tantrum to get to me. Something deep in my chest aches and warms at the same time from hearing this. I want to give him another chance, but I wonder if the damage has already been done. His lies are a lot to take in, but he had no choice at the time but to lie to me.

"How is Cori?"

The look that crosses the nurse's face makes me fear the worst. I don't know what to expect and have no idea if I will be able to live with myself if something happens to her. She is my bestie, my family and so like a sister to me that I don't think I could survive without her.

"Well, she is in a medically induced coma until some of her injuries heal. I can take you to her in a few minutes if you want."

"Yes, thank you. What are her injuries?"

"Well, she listed you as next of kin so I can get her doctor to meet us there so he can talk to you. I am not all that familiar with her injuries except for hearsay."

Not surprising that she listed me as next of kin, Cori doesn't have a lot of family. I still wish I had someone to call to let them know about her. She deserves love, hell she deserves all the love in the world. Hopefully one day she will find it if she pulls through. Just thinking about her in a coma because of me just makes me hate myself even more.

"Let me go page the doc, and then I will come in and help you get yourself together so you can see her. I'll be right back." She is entirely too bubbly and chipper. She has fiery red hair and the personality to match.

I almost scream out in pain trying to scoot to the side of the bed, but I keep it together. Kimberly comes in and walks me to the bathroom. I'm sore and stiff but, all in all, ok. Until I look in the mirror. Bruises dot my face and line my jaw, my hair looks like a family of rats have taken up residence on my head. My breath is enough to knock someone over, and don't even get me started on my lack of a shower in quite a few days.

Kimberly yells through the door that I have a care package that someone brought me with shampoo, a change of clothes and all the fixings. I send a silent thanks into the air to whoever sent it because I am desperate right now. I feel like my teeth have fuzzy stuff growing on them.

After a shower, I feel semi-human. I don't think it was my mom that left me the stuff because she knows what shampoo I use and this one was too high end for my tastes. But I certainly won't complain. The clothes are brand new as well, just a white t-shirt and drawstring pants, which is a welcome thing because I was scared to have to put jeans on. The pain from that would certainly ruin the good shower I just had.

Running the brush through my hair is too hard, so when I stick my head out of the bathroom door expecting to see Kimberly, seeing Damian is a shock. But my goodness, he looks amazing.

"Need some help?" His hands are in his pockets and he leans up against the foot of the bed. His gun is strapped to his side.

"Yeah, I need my hair brushed. Can you get Kimberly for me?"

"I can do it if you will let me."

He stares directly into my eyes and it is hard to think of anything else other than the way he felt when he was inside of me. He goes to sit higher up on the bed and pats the spot in front of him. I walk towards him and it feels like I am approaching the firing squad. Maybe just the firing squad for my heart, because thinking back, he was never bad to me. He never hurt me physically, sure he lied to me, but it was a part of his job. He made me believe that he worked for Xavier, but he had to. I feel like I can't breathe. I feel like he has x-ray vision and when I look into his eyes he can see deep down into my thoughts. Just thinking of that has me giggling and he gives me a curious stare.

"It was nothing." He gives me a look like yeah, right.

After sitting and getting myself into a position that doesn't hurt, he gathers my hair into his hand. I swear every time he brushes my neck with his fingers I about come on the spot. I can feel the wetness pooling in my new panties. I feel my body temperature rising, and I wonder if he can feel it as well. He is gentle in his brushing, and I couldn't be more thankful for that. With the knots finally detangled I find that I don't want to leave this spot. His legs are up against my thighs and I can feel the muscles flex with his every movement. I can feel his erection through his pants, resting up against my back, letting me know he is just as turned on as I am.

I whisper out a shy 'thank you' and he clears his throat before delivering a very gruff 'welcome.' His hands barely skim my side and I cannot help it, I moan. I feel his erection pulse, almost like a bounce up against my back. Grabbing a hold of my hair in one hand he pulls my head back. I don't feel any pain only pleasure.

"Tell me you forgive me, Livvy baby. Tell me you want to see where this goes. Tell me," he demands, his voice a sultry plea.

I try to nod my head yes, but he doesn't let me. Instead, he whispers in the shell of my ear. "No baby, tell me." His lips barely skim the outside of my ear and my whole body breaks out in goosebumps.

"I do."

"You do what, Livvy baby?"

"I forgive you."

"Good."

With that, he turns my head so I can see him and he kisses me. Exploring each other's mouths with tongues and teeth. Setting each other on fire with the want and need to explore. Sucking my bottom lip into his mouth, I moan as if releasing some of this sound will help with the pressure I feel to have him inside of me. I reach down to pull his t-shirt over his head, forgetting that we are in a hospital room because all I want to feel is his skin on mine. To absorb his heat into me. But when I start pulling and my hand touches his gun it is like a bucket of ice cold water being thrown on me. I bring my head down to rest on his chin and try to cool my raging libido.

"I need to go see Cori."

"Ok, I'll take you. I have been visiting with her when Jack and your mom were here. I know you wouldn't want your friend alone."

I feel the tears spring to my eyes, but I try to blink them away. I don't want to be a blubbering mess after I just had a shower. Hand in hand we walk towards her room. It is a slow walk since I am still stiff and sore, but he never complains. Not once did he try to drag me along, he just slows his pace waiting for me.

Arriving the ICU, I was not prepared for what I would see. I don't really think any amount of preparation would have prepared me. She has bandages all over her face, across her forehead and cheeks. I rush to her side and reach out to hold her hand but stop myself. She probably hates me, I hate me. Good people are dead because of me, and she almost died.

"Miss Ambrose, I'm Dr. Brinkley, Cori's doctor. I know this is a shock to see her this way, but I can assure you she is comfortable and not in pain. Unfortunately, we had to put her in a medically induced coma to let some of her injuries heal."

"Tell me about them."

He rubs the back of his neck and looks from me to Damian. Damian gives a slight head nod towards the doc.

"Well, she suffered major facial lacerations, the result of cutting in the shape of an X. She had several bruised organs and three broken ribs. She also had some vaginal lacerations consistent with being raped. We will be waking her in the next few days. Do you have any questions?"

"Yes, what about STDs or anything like that? Also, how many stitches? How long is her recovery time?"

"We did a rapid HIV test which came back negative along with the rest of the STD panel. Hepatitis was also negative. As far as stitches go, she received all in all 216 on her face, 6 on her vagina to close the tears. Her recovery time physically will vary within a few months. Emotionally and mentally, no way of telling how long. In all honesty, it is a surprise that she survived. But she is certainly a fighter, her biggest fight will be soon, though."

With that, he walks out of the room and all I can do is stare at her. This was all my fault, I caused this, and I am the one to blame. She will hate me when she wakes up and rightfully so. Swiping at the tears that have fallen, I go to her and hold her hand, they look so small. Whispering in her ear, I hope that she knows how sorry I am.

Damian comes up behind me and puts a hand on my shoulder, it is meant to be comforting, but in reality it makes me feel worse. Here I am with this gorgeous man, I escaped with a few bruises and a concussion, and here she is broken. I will do everything within my power to help her heal if she will let me.

"Livvy baby, come on. Let's go back to your room. Jack and your mom should be here soon."

Seeing my questioning look, he says that he saw Mom and Jack in the waiting room and they said they were going to get some food for us.

I guess being asleep for a few days and my mom and Jack meeting Damian has helped me skip the hard introductions. I just wonder how Jack and my mom really feel about him. Nervous butterflies take up residence in my belly the entire walk back to my room. Walking in, I see Mom and Jack waiting for us. They brought lunch for all of us, and we all eat in somewhat silence. Jack, of course, is the only one gabbing away to Damian about his favorite wrestler. Damian listens intently and asks questions when needed. Our eyes lock and he winks at me. Immediate flood in my panties. Hearing snickering, I look at my mom.

"What?"

"Oh nothing, but you guys got it bad! I have never seen you look at someone this way, not even when you were with Jack's dad. It is a good thing, Olivia, you deserve a man that worships you and Jack. You deserve one who takes your breath away. I think he will be good for you. Besides, Jack has definitely taken a shine to him. I like him as well. I have been worried about you, girl. You seem to have lost how to be a woman in her 20's. You became a mom and it all stopped with that. You have done a beautiful job raising my grandson, but now it is time for you to find you. Find your happiness, find your forever after."

DAMIAN

Is this what a family looks like? Obviously not sitting in a hospital room, but sharing a meal and talking to each other about everything and nothing at all. I don't know, but I can't wait to find out. I never thought I would settle down and be true to one woman. I never wanted to, never needed to. But now feeling this, I can't believe I never wanted it for myself.

Looking at this boy, this magnetic, overly talkative boy and I feel like I am lucky to be in his presence. He is definitely a special kid, one who has just the best parts of Livvy in him which, of course, is everything. Ladies need to watch out, and Dads need to shield their daughters for when this guy gets dating age. I can't wait to see it. Wait, what? What makes me think that I will be around that long?

Thinking about being around in the long term fills me with a warmth I never thought was possible. Gives me a feeling of hope that I never knew I needed. Could I possibly be more to them? A husband? A dad? I don't know if I can, but I know that I want to.

Epilogue
Olivia

It has been 3 weeks since I was released from the hospital. I have been to 5 funerals since I got out. Mary, the Warden, Burton and 2 other guards. Cori is awake and healing, but she is closed off from me. She tells me that she doesn't blame me and she doesn't hate me, but I'm not sure.

Sitting in the bathroom waiting it is all I can think about. Life changes and all we can do is hold on and not fly off. The beep of the kitchen timer brings my attention back to the here and now. Oh shit! What the hell am I going to do? How in the hell can I be fucking pregnant? Damian is going to shit himself. He is trying so hard to be what we need and want. I don't know if he can handle this on top of everything.

Walking out of the bathroom I see the 2 men in my life playing basketball in the backyard. I'm nervous and scared to tell Damian, but he needs to know.

Holding the test in my hand, I walk out into the back yard to hear them trash talking each other.

"Brick!" I hear my son yell out. Damian laughs at his trash talk. They don't even stop when they both see me.

"Hey J, can you go inside? I need to talk to D for a minute." Jack and Damian have started calling each other by their first initials, something Damian started, now Jack calls everyone by theirs.

"Sure thing M, besides, he was losing anyways." With that, he takes off running.

I set the test down on the table on the back patio. I see him eye it, then I see the second the recognition hits.

"Are you? Are we?"

"Apparently so."

I never expected him to cheer and pick me up and twirl me. I also never expected him to drop down on one knee.

"Livvy baby, I know it has only been 3 weeks, I know that people will think we are rushing it. But my heart calls to your heart, it seeks yours out when we are apart. In just 3 short weeks, we have been through a lifetime of struggle but I can promise you that if you give me forever, we will never struggle again. If you give me forever, I will be the best dad to Jack and this baby that there ever was. You will want for nothing, Livvy baby, will you please do me the honor of being my wife. The honor of being my forever, of being the other half of my heart. Because, baby, when I am not with you, my heart doesn't seem to beat. I can't seem to breathe when you are not here. So what do you say?"

"Yes, yes, yes I will marry you! I can't believe this."

Sliding the beautiful princess cut diamond on my finger makes me think of how happy I am, also makes me think of how bad it could have been.

Before Damian puts me down, my mom and Jack run outside clapping. Jack rushes over to Damian and he sets my feet the ground before kneeling down eye level with Jack.

"So are you goiing to be my dad?" Jack asks, his voice laced with hope and admiration.

"Always bud, I will always be your dad."

Acknowledgments

To my husband who always told me I should do it but I was too big of a pain in the ass to actually do it. But hey, I did it!

To Corinne…You're my twin sista from another mista! Your friendship has meant more to me in the past year than you realize!

I would say to my kiddos, but I always found that weird in a romance book.

To my bonus dad, Eddie, whom we lost in May of 2015. He was the perfect bonus to my crazy family and I miss him more and more all the time. I hope that I have made him proud of me.

Dawn, Dawn, Glenna, Chelsea and Amanda, you ladies are the definition of rock stars! Your guidance and hand holding through all of this has been amazing and I could never repay you for your encouragement.

For all my haters in the world. Hold on, there is TONS more to come, so if you haven't hated on me, be patient, I won't disappoint!

To Silla Webb, you have been an amazing editor, cover designer, formatter, promoter, and all around person. I share whatever success may come with you!

Doodle, I acknowledge how big of an ass dog you are. Literally.

To any readers of this book, I thank you for taking the time to read it! This has certainly been a labor of love and I hope you love these two as much as I do. Thank you from the top of my head to the tips of my toes. Without you and your reviews, none of us indies would be where we are. YOU, the reader are rock stars in my mind!

Meet Renee

Renee Adams is a wannabe spunky girl who is generally too tired to be spunky! She hails all the way from NC but spent most of her life in VA. When she is not writing, she is spending time with her 2 kids, husband and Doodle the dog. She also accomplished her dreams of becoming a nurse and working in a prison, but since enjoys staying at home and keeping her family in line and providing lots of laughter. You can find her on Facebook where she posts her Spam Email of the Day, or on the Twitter @homeskilletbsct. She cracks herself up and more often than not is off posting memes somewhere.

Stalk her on Facebook

https://www.facebook.com/authorreneeadams

Twitter

@homeskilletbsct

Or Goodreads

https://www.goodreads.com/author/show/14427753.Renee_Adams

Printed in Great Britain
by Amazon